DEAD Lil' HUSTLER

VICTORIA HOUSTON

TYRUS
BOOKS

F+W Media, Inc.

Published by TYRUS BOOKS
an imprint of F+W Media, Inc.
10151 Carver Road, Suite 200
Blue Ash, OH 45242. U.S.A.
www.tyrusbooks.com

Hardcover ISBN 10: 1-4405-6841-3
Hardcover ISBN 13: 978-1-4405-6841-1
Paperback ISBN 10: 1-4405-6840-5
Paperback ISBN 13: 978-1-4405-6840-4
eISBN 10: 1-4405-6842-1
eISBN 13: 978-1-4405-6842-8

Printed in the United States of America.

10 9 8 7 6 5 4 3 2 1

This is a work of fiction. Names, characters, corporations, institutions, organizations, events, or locales in this novel are either the product of the author's imagination or, if real, used fictitiously. The resemblance of any character to actual persons (living or dead) is entirely coincidental.

Many of the designations used by manufacturers and sellers to distinguish their product are claimed as trademarks. Where those designations appear in this book and F+W Media, Inc. was aware of a trademark claim, the designations have been printed with initial capital letters.

Cover design by Sylvia McArdle.
Cover images © 123RF/Paco Ayala/Shirley Zedar.
Author photo courtesy of Marcha Moore.

*This book is available at quantity discounts for bulk purchases.
For information, please call 1-800-289-0963.*

For Riley, Willow, Quinlan, and Todd—who were there
with love and humor when it counted

"You can tell the nature of a man from his companion or his wife. Every woman explains the man by whom she is loved, and vice versa: he explains her character."

—ODILON REDON, 1869

Chapter One

Easing the beat-up SUV to the side of the road, Liam Barber reached behind his seat for the tattered copy of the *Wisconsin Gazetteer*. He ran his finger down the grid, then turned to the corresponding page with the topographic map showing where the Pine River narrowed to what was likely a barely navigable stream: perfect for trout. The map indicated that the stream jogged to the left just short of the dirt road he had passed moments ago. He was pretty sure he had to be close to the right spot but he checked the page once again. Well . . . he might be off by a few yards but it was worth a try.

He glanced at his watch. If he started right now he'd have his entire lunch hour to explore the area.

He still couldn't believe he had landed the perfect summer internship collecting samples of invasive plant species, a job that guaranteed he'd be able to work outdoors. And get *paid*. They might make him drive this crummy car but what the heck—this would be one great summer.

Professor Cruikshank in the UW Botany Department had gone on and on about the native brook trout that could be found in the shaded, cold streams running through the Nicolet National Forest. Because the streams were hidden so deep in the woods, few people fished them.

That will not be me, thought Liam. He was young and strong and ready for the challenge: Secret water can mean superb fishing.

Pulling on his fishing vest, Liam checked the pockets to be sure he had his sandwich, his compass, and the hand-carved wooden fly box. The box held two dry flies—one resembled a Royal Wulff and the other a foam hopper-type pattern.

Both trout flies had been tied by Takumi Tsuchiya, a friend he had met in Japan and a fly-fisherman who had taught him the art of tenkara fly-fishing. Liam had met Takumi during the year he spent teaching English as a second language in Japan. Upon learning that Liam loved to fly-fish Takumi had insisted he learn the Japanese style of fly-fishing: tenkara.

Awed by the simplicity of tenkara with its rod, line, and dry fly—no reel—Liam had become so enthralled by the sport that during a vacation back in the States he had insisted that his father, Jake, learn tenkara as well. After all, it was Jake who had spurred his son's addiction to traditional fly-fishing when he turned ten.

Earlier that summer, the two of them had spent hours fishing their way upstream from their cabin in Wyoming before Liam flew to northern Wisconsin to take the job. Liam had taken the lead, showing his father that tenkara was not about the cast (which both men had spent way too much time stressing over) but about the trout fly and what you want it to do once you have oh so delicately dropped it onto the surface of the stream.

"Dad, no—the goal is to be *one* with your trout fly—not hammer it," Liam admonished every time Jake tried to power through his cast with the long, unfamiliar tenkara fly rod. "Keep it simple . . . intuitive . . ."

"Maybe it's too Zen for me," Jake had said, frustrated at first. But he caught on and before long father and son found tenkara to be a fine way to spend time in the water, time together.

Today marked two weeks since Liam had been able to carve out time for fishing. Frankly, he thought, after the hours he had put in scouring the forest floor for invasive plant species, he deserved at least an hour in the stream. An hour with his tenkara rod, his trout fly, the burbling waters, and the Dresden blue sky: just one hour of heaven and he would be happy.

After double-checking to be sure that the delicate, handmade wooden fly box that Takumi had given him was stowed safely in his pocket, Liam gathered up his gear. Gear? He had to chuckle. Tenkara gear is basic beyond belief and so easy to carry: two trout flies and a fourteen-foot collapsible rod with twelve feet of fifteen-pound-test fluorocarbon plus three feet of 5X tippet. And no reel. Perfect for someone planning to bushwhack into backcountry.

Ready for action, Liam crossed the road, stumbled down the grassy slope to the ditch, then up the other side and into the woods. About a hundred yards in he paused to listen. Yes! He could hear water. He stepped up his pace. The July sun was high overhead but the air under the forest canopy was cool.

In less than ten minutes he found himself on the edge of a swampy patch of tag alder beyond which was a boulder-strewn stream. Just what he had hoped to find. He reached for his rod case and uncapped it.

Then he set the rod case down and, rod in hand, stepped into the water, which was so cold he wished he had brought his waders along. Oh well. He glanced upstream: perfect. It might be called a "river" but the Pine along this stretch was just a stream—and what a lovely stream, the current racing past and around huge boulders and misshapen rocks that would provide the riffles and pools ideal for hidden caches of wild trout.

He moved forward studying the rocky terrain. He liked how narrow the stream was. That would make it easy for his long tenkara rod to reach across the rippling currents and drop his kebari—the word Takumi used to mean "trout fly"—into one of the quiet pools hiding behind one of the boulders. When he had reached a stretch that struck him as ideal for his first cast, he leaned back against a large boulder and pulled from the pocket of his cargo shorts the spool holding his line. He attached the line to the tip of the rod, then unfurled it, testing the tippet on the end before tying on his kebari.

He always used the same kebari—in fact, his tenkara trout fly was a Royal Wulff dry fly—the one trout fly he could tie himself and be satisfied with. That was something else that Takumi had taught him: Tenkara fishing is not like its American cousin where "matching the hatch" is mandatory. No, no, no. The tenkara fisherman is concerned with one thing only—the *presentation* of the trout fly. As in Zen Buddhism where a person seeks to be at one with his breath, at one with the moment in which he is living, so is tenkara about being focused on the kebari floating in the stillness behind the big rock.

When his rod and line and kebari were ready, Liam stood up and walked upstream another few yards to where he could see a silence of water beckoning from behind a black rock cantilevered over burbling stones. Before making a move with his rod, he turned his face up for a caress from the warm July sun. Whispers from the tag alders lining the riverbank were as friendly as the smile he'd gotten from the girl he hoped to ask out later that day. He lifted his rod and, leaning forward, sent the kebari over the rock and into the pool. He waited. He watched the still water, the drifting kebari, his universe . . . a pause in the movement of the kebari. Liam struck.

His rod bent as the fish fought but the tippet did not break. Minutes passed before the fish stopped struggling. Liam pulled the sparkling beauty of a brook trout into the shallow water at his feet. With gentle hands he retrieved his kebari then slipped the brookie back into the stream.

Satisfied, he walked over to a grassy hummock and was sitting down to savor the moment when his jaw disintegrated. The second bullet slammed into the back of his neck. He died in the embrace of a tag alder.

Chapter Two

Four Days Later

"Hey, Dad," said Erin, her voice breaking up over Paul Osborne's cell phone. "Are you . . . busy?"

"Am I busy? Hard to hear you, kid. Can you hear me?"

"Now I can," said Erin. "Sorry, I must have hit a dead zone. I was wondering if you're busy right now?"

"Just leaving the house," said Osborne. "Rushing Mike to the vet. He got into it with a porcupine last night—not sure I got all the quills out."

"Oh, good, you'll be in town. I mean, sorry about the dog but since you're going to be in town—"

Osborne could hear anxiety in her voice. "What do you need?"

"Would you mind stopping by the house to check on Cody? He wasn't feeling well this morning and I had to leave early to drive down to Wausau for a client meeting. Mark's got court today and both girls had sleepovers at friends' houses last night. Do you mind? It's just a bad cold but he looked so sad when I left."

"C'mon, you know how I hate that kid," teased Osborne, smiling to himself. "Of course I'll check on the little guy. Right after we see the vet. Mind if I bring him out to my place? He can help me clean up around the dock, maybe we'll drown a few worms—no better medicine than July sunshine."

Erin chuckled as she said, "Sure, Dad, any excuse to use that new pontoon, right?"

"Well, I bought it for you and the kids." And he had. The pontoon was quite small, designed to be transported on a standard boat trailer, and to hold no more than four people. In Osborne's mind ever since he had retired from his dental practice the four included himself and his three grandchildren, although the oldest, Beth, was hitting her teens and more interested in boys than fishing. Funny how that happens.

Ten-year-old Mason could be counted on to enjoy spending time on the lake but it was Cody, who had just turned seven and was showing promise of being as tall and lanky and as smitten with the outdoors as his grandfather, who begged his mom daily to "drop me off at Grandpa's—he needs help with that new boat."

After the vet had determined that Mike would survive the two remaining porcupine quills he was able to remove, Osborne pulled up in front of the big yellow Victorian where his youngest daughter and her family lived. The day was so warm that he rolled down all the windows and opened the Subaru's tailgate. He wanted to be sure the breezes could reach the black lab resting in his crate. "Be right back, Mike. Watch the car."

He ran up the front steps of the house and onto the porch. He peered through the screen door into the living room. "Cody?"

"Grandpa?" A weak voice answered him. Osborne opened the door and walked in. His grandson was lying on a couch in the living room, a light blue coverlet pulled up to his shoulders and a glass of water with a straw on the floor beside the couch. On the end table behind Cody's head was a plate of cookies that appeared to be untouched. A thermometer rested on a paper towel.

Kneeling beside the boy, Osborne laid the back of his right hand against the child's forehead. "Whoa, son, you are hot," he said, noting how flushed the child's face was.

"No I'm not," whispered Cody, pulling at the coverlet and shivering as he spoke. "Grandpa, I'm freezing." He was shivering so violently his teeth chattered.

"I see that." Tucking the blanket tight around Cody's shoulders, Osborne sat back on his heels to study the child. Something wasn't right. It had to be over 80 degrees in the room—why was he so cold? A memory nagged at the back of his mind followed by a surge of adrenaline shot with fear.

"Anything hurt?" Osborne got to his feet.

"My head. My head hurts real bad." Cody closed his eyes as he kept shivering.

"Headache, huh. Feel dizzy?"

"Kinda."

"Okay, kiddo," said Osborne as he reached to scoop Cody up by the shoulders. "I want you to sit up here. We're going to check something."

He pulled Cody into a sitting position so that he was on the edge of the sofa facing forward with his bare feet on the floor. Placing one hand gently against the child's back, Osborne said, "Cody, I want you to touch your chin to your chest."

The child made a slight movement. "Ooh . . . I can't." Cody looked at his grandfather with tears in his eyes. "It hurts."

Osborne reached into his shirt pocket for his cell phone and dialed 911. "I need the number for St. Mary's Emergency Room," he said to the dispatcher who answered.

"Dr. Osborne?" asked a familiar voice.

"Dani? You're working today?"

Dani Wright cobbled together two jobs as she studied for a degree in law enforcement at the local tech college. She worked part-time as the IT tech for the Loon Lake Police Department and, whenever they needed someone, as a 911 dispatcher for the county sheriff's department.

"Yes. Are you okay, Doc?"

"I'm fine but I have a very sick grandchild and I need that phone number."

"Here it is." She repeated the number twice to be sure he had it.

On reaching the emergency room nurse taking calls, Osborne spoke fast. He gave his name and Cody's and said that he was rushing over "with a very sick little boy. Please have someone meet us out front." He didn't wait for a response but clicked off.

Squeezing his grandson's shoulder, he said, "I'll be right back, Cody. Just need to put Mike in the backyard. Don't worry, little guy. Everything will be okay."

Osborne dashed down the front steps, opened the crate for Mike to jump out, and hustled the dog along the side of the house and through a side gate to the backyard. Two members of Erin's family were waiting: Lucy, an aging golden retriever, and Barney, their new dachshund pup. The dogs looked up with interest at Mike's unexpected arrival. After checking to be sure the dogs had plenty of water, Osborne ran up the back stairs leading to the kitchen.

He wrapped the coverlet tight around Cody and swept him up in both arms. With Cody's head cradled against his chest, Osborne could sense how weak the child was. After carefully laying the boy down on the back seat of the Subaru, he sped through the streets of Loon Lake to the hospital's emergency entrance.

Two blocks from the hospital his cell phone rang. "Doc, Dani just called me," said Lewellyn Ferris, Loon Lake's Chief of Police. "Who's sick? One of the girls?"

"Cody. Could be spinal meningitis. Can't talk now. I'm almost to the hospital. Wait, one thing, Lew. Mark's in court—can you reach him and tell him to meet me here? And he needs to call Erin." Osborne's voice cracked.

"Done."

• • •

During the three years that they had been seeing each other, Lewellyn Ferris and Paul Osborne had found themselves sharing memories of the most difficult times in their lives. For Lew, it was a hot August night when her only son was knifed in a bar fight. He died instantly. For Osborne, it was the winter afternoon when his mother turned deathly ill.

He was six years old, his mother just twenty-eight. He could remember the day, hour by hour, when she had fallen ill with a high fever and dizziness. Little kid that he was, he tried his best to help but there was little he could do except bring cold washcloths for her forehead. Insisting it was "only a flu," she refused to call a doctor until his father got home. But his father was away at the Wisconsin State Dental Society's annual meeting and not due back until the next day.

By the time Dr. Osborne, Sr. had returned and was able to rush her to the hospital, it was too late—the meningitis had escalated into encephalitis. Within forty-eight hours she was dead. Since that day, Osborne acknowledged that the meningococcal bacterial infection was not common and his worry was unreasonable—but he lived in such fear of spinal meningitis that he would apologize to his daughters' pediatricians for bothering them every time one of his girls ran a high fever.

Chapter Three

"Follow me, please, Dr. Osborne," said the admitting clerk on the emergency desk, motioning for Osborne, Cody cradled in his arms, to follow her to a small waiting room with a gurney. No doctor in sight.

Osborne could feel his blood pressure rise as he asked, "Why are we in here? This child needs immediate medical attention. I called ahead for one of the trauma docs to meet us—"

"One of the team should be here shortly," said the clerk, her voice flat. She turned and left.

Resigned for the moment, Osborne whispered, "Gently, gently, little guy," as he bent to lay Cody on the gurney, tuck the coverlet around him, and smooth the child's hair back from his hot forehead.

Sitting down on the one chair in the room, he waited. He checked his watch. Five minutes had passed since he walked through the automatic doors to the emergency room. He checked his watch again. Okay, he'd give it five more minutes. No. More.

At a rustling of the coverlet, Osborne scrambled to his feet. He looked down to see Cody's teeth clenched and grinding from side to side. A second later the boy's body went rigid.

Racing into the hall, Osborne shouted, "Help! He's convulsing. Please, someone, help!"

Two nurses in blue scrubs came running out of nearby rooms.

"My grandson—he's having a seizure," said Osborne, pointing at the open door behind him. "Get a doctor. *Now.*"

The first nurse hurried into the room and leaned over Cody. "Looks okay to me."

"A moment ago, he had a seizure," said Osborne, struggling to control his fury. "I was a dentist for thirty years. I know a goddamn seizure when I see one. This is my grandson and I can tell you I *know* he had a seizure."

Before the nurse could reply, a young physician rushed into the room. Osborne closed his eyes, took a deep breath, and tried to calm down. He told the doctor, "I know I'm overreacting but my mother died of spinal meningitis and these symptoms, Doctor . . ."

"I understand. I'm on the trauma unit, I know what to look for," said the physician who appeared to be all of twelve years old. After checking Cody's vital signs, he had the child sit up and try to touch his chin to his chest. Meantime, the first nurse had left and a second arrived to take her place.

Standing with his back to Osborne, the doctor spoke in a low tone to the nurse, "We need to move him to the ICU Isolation unit until we know if this is viral or bacterial. I'll need tests run ASAP. Get someone else to cover other patients coming into ER."

He turned to face Osborne. "Dr. Osborne, I'm Dr. Schrieber. I'll be attending your grandson. Please, the waiting room is right around the corner. I'll keep you fully informed but right now—"

"I'll get out of the way," said Osborne with a wave of his hand. "I have to reach his parents."

Entering the waiting area, Osborne spotted Lew across the room talking with his son-in-law, Mark. He started toward them but before he had taken two steps, a tall, heavyset man blocked his way. "Hey, Doc, what's up? You in for brain surgery? Always knew you had a screw loose."

One look at Osborne's face and Bud Jarvison backed off. "Sorry. Anything serious?"

"Later, Bud."

"Okay, Doc. I'll be here—got the old lady in recovering from surgery. Later, then, and sorry for the intrusion," said Bud as he dropped his weight into a nearby chair.

A hulking, loquacious man with an alcohol nose, Bud had a habit of greeting Osborne as if he were his best buddy—until someone more important showed up. It had been that way since childhood. Osborne usually managed to find a polite way to exit whenever he ran into the guy. Today he had no time for good manners.

Relieved to get by Bud with no small talk, Osborne motioned for Lew and Mark to follow him into the hall and out of earshot of the people in the waiting room.

"I reached Erin on her way back from Wausau. She should be here any minute," said Mark. "How bad is it?"

"Not sure yet. The doctor is running tests right now. I'm afraid it is meningitis but whether it's bacterial or viral—we don't know yet."

"What difference does that make?" asked Lew.

"Bacterial can be treated with antibiotics, viral has to run its course. We have to hope that it's viral—even with antibiotics bacterial can be deadly. That's what my mother died of."

"What's going on, Dad?" Erin ran toward them with a look that should never visit the face of a mother. "Dad? Mark?" As she neared, she burst into tears. "What on earth? What did I do? Oh, my God . . ."

"Hey, hey, hold on," said Osborne, folding his arms around his daughter. "You didn't do anything. I'm sure Cody was not that sick when you left. But by the time I got there, his temperature had skyrocketed."

Dr. Schrieber appeared in the hallway. "Are you the boy's parents?" he asked Mark and Erin. "Come with me. You, too, Dr. Osborne."

"I'll wait here," said Lew. Osborne nodded and followed the trio down the hall into a small office.

"Mr. and Mrs. Amundson, Dr. Osborne," said the physician. "Here is all we know right now. Meningitis is an inflammation of the lining that surrounds the spinal cord and the brain. Symptoms can come on so fast and seem so ordinary—fever, headache, stiff neck, and a rash. You may have thought it was just a cold or flu," he said to Erin. "I would have thought the same if one of my kids looked like that earlier today. Has anyone else in the home or your neighbors been sick recently?"

"Yes, some of the boys on Cody's T-ball team have had the mumps," said Erin.

"That could be it," said the doctor. "Could be a virus hit your son's immune system and it reacted this way. We'll be running tests to see what we have. Meantime, we have to keep Cody in isolation because we may not know for several days . . ."

"Know what? How many days?" asked Mark.

"Not sure, five, six maybe."

"But you won't know *what?*" asked Erin.

The doctor paused, then said, "If he'll make it. Your son is a very sick little boy. All we can do right now is keep him stable. There are a number of different strains of meningitis. Some we can treat, some not. The risks run from hearing loss to brain damage to limbs that may need to be amputated."

"That bad," said Erin, trying hard to keep her composure. "That bad, really?"

"I wish I could tell you more. We're bringing in a specialist from Madison and he may be able to answer your questions better than I can. Oh, one question—I have two residents on the team who are studying infectious diseases. Do you mind if they run some additional tests? They will meet with you first and tell you what and why."

"Anything. Everything," said Erin, trying to talk through her tears.

Mark put an arm around his wife. "Can we see him?"

• • •

Osborne left the office and walked back to the waiting room. With a quick glance through the doorway he could see Bud Jarvison still parked in an easy chair near the magazine rack. Once again he motioned for Lew to join him in the hall. The last person he needed asking questions right now was Bud.

"Lew," said Osborne. "They don't know how sick Cody is. Could be . . ." A sudden pressure of tears made it difficult for Osborne to continue. Lew put a comforting arm around his waist and waited. "Well, it's not good. Some strain of meningitis and we have to hope that it's viral. If it's bacterial . . ." Again Osborne choked up, pressing his fingers against his eyelids.

Watching his face, Lew could tell the news was everything he did not want to hear. She also knew how helpless he must feel. "Would you like me to stay, Doc? Until you know more."

Osborne inhaled deeply, "No, this could take a while, Lew. You have a police department to run."

"Things can be canceled . . ." She pursed her lips as she looked up at him.

"Really?" Osborne managed a small smile. "You can tell a bunch of jabones to put their bad behavior on hold?"

"Well, no, but I can ask Todd to take over for a while."

"No, Lew, it's okay. You can go."

She squeezed his hand and stood on her tiptoes to give him a peck on the cheek. "Call if you need me, okay?"

"Thanks, I will." As she walked off, Osborne watched her go, thinking as he often did these days how lucky he was that she had invited him into her life.

He turned around to find Bud standing at the entrance to the waiting room, hands on his hips and his big head thrust forward. "I didn't know you knew Chief Ferris, Doc," said Bud. The knowing grin on his face irritated Osborne. "How long has this been going on? What have I missed?"

"It's business, Bud, all business," said Osborne with a dismissive wave. "For the last couple years, I've been asked to fill in for Pecore when he's, ah, you know, out of sorts as they say. You know what I mean—on occasion. The county and the police department like to have a health professional as coroner when they can and I have the time so—there it is."

The grin hadn't left Bud's face so Osborne heard himself rattle on, "I had to call 911 this morning and Chief Ferris wanted to be sure that there hadn't been an accident—that's all."

"You called 911?" asked Bud, raising his eyebrows.

"Yeah, my grandson's got some virus or something. Not sure, yet. No big deal, Bud."

Heading toward the exit, Osborne gave a weak grin and waved goodbye, hoping that would satisfy Bud, for the moment at least.

Chapter Four

After the race to the emergency room with the siren on and lights flashing, Lew decided to take her time driving back to the station. She wanted time to think over the crisis facing Doc and his family.

How could the life of that rambunctious little boy be in such danger? And without warning? One minute he's a child coming down with a cold and then . . .

A crackle from the police radio interrupted her thoughts.

"Chief Ferris? Dani, here. I'm back at the station—is Dr. Osborne's grandson okay?"

"They're running tests," said Lew. "See you in a minute, Dani, I'm only a few blocks away—"

"That's why I radioed, Chief. The Forestry Service called in a few minutes ago. Two kayakers found a body in the Pine River. Sounds like it's in bad shape—like really dead. Y'know—like bones and all?"

Lew couldn't help getting a kick out of Dani's take on some of the situations that the police had to deal with. The young woman had never considered herself a candidate for police work but after being assigned to help the Loon Lake Police with an investigation at the local tech college, she surprised everyone, including herself, with a natural talent for using the computer for advanced searches and data analysis.

"I'm a geek and I never knew it," she had laughed when praised for using the computer to locate the source of criminal activity on the college campus.

It didn't take much for Lew to convince her she had a future on the investigative team. Although the nineteen-year-old changed her major at the tech college from cosmetics to law enforcement, she had not lost her less-than-sophisticated perspective on dead bodies.

"Yeah, so, at first the ranger who took the call thought they must have found a dead bear but the kayakers told him bears don't wear snowmobile suits so—"

"Okay, okay," said Lew with a sigh. "I'll get Pecore on the line and have him meet me there. Do you have an exact location?"

"Yes, I do," said Dani.

Lew pulled over to jot down the directions.

"Damn," she said to herself as she scrolled through the numbers on her cell phone looking for Pecore's home number. Wasn't the day bad enough without being forced to work with that razzbonya?

Thanks to his brother-in-law, Loon Lake's longtime mayor, Pecore had been appointed Loon Lake's coroner in perpetuity or, at least, until the mayor expired. This was in spite of the fact that his prior work experience was limited to running a tavern—though which side of the bar he preferred was a subject for debate among many Loon Lake citizens.

Worse had been Pecore's longtime habit under the former chief of police of letting his two golden retrievers into the coroner's office and its long-out-of-date small morgue where bodies had once been stored until identified. More than once the dogs had been seen nosing around the shelves holding evidence bags—thus violating the chain of custody and compromising more than one criminal case. The nightmare among some Loon Lake families had been that the dogs may have had access to the dearly departed stored nearby.

Outraged when she heard about Pecore's habits—and after being promoted to Chief—Lew had been able to limit his access to evidence and the bodies of the deceased. Given he was not a pathologist, she effected a policy change that ensured that the bodies of any victims not claimed by families were now stored in the hospital morgue before being sent south for autopsies.

Time and again Lew had argued that Pecore should be replaced by someone with credentials in the health-care field, each time struggling to find a nice way to say that the man was so incompetent she worried he would declare a live person "dead"— and get them all sued.

These days the one redeeming factor for Loon Lake's Police Chief Lewellyn Ferris was Pecore's habit of spending a good chunk of his days and most of his nights so over-served that she had a handy excuse for deputizing a certain retired dentist to step in for him. Pecore didn't mind—he was salaried.

But this was no day to ask Doc to help out.

Punching Pecore's home number into her phone, Lew sighed as she waited for the usual voicemail. Neither Pecore nor his wife believed in answering their phone. If they didn't pick up, she decided after two rings, she would drive right over to his house and physically tear numbnut away from the *History Channel.* All he had to do today was declare a poor soul dead who had been in the water for months. She hoped he could rise to the occasion for once. It was ten in the morning but this wouldn't be the first time she might find him on his fourth or fifth beer.

To her surprise a cheery male voice answered. *Cheery and sober.* "Hello, this is Ed Pecore—is this Dr. Portman?"

"Sorry, Pecore, this is Chief Ferris. Who's Dr. Portman?"

"Oh." The disappointment in Pecore's voice was palpable. "He's my orthopod, what's up?"

Lew couldn't help but notice how quickly he changed the subject.

"I'm calling because I need the services of our trusty Loon Lake coroner this morning," she said, trying hard to sound friendly. "Couple kayakers just called in saying they found a body in the Pine River over in the national forest. Sounds like a snowmobiler who went through the ice a few months ago—so be prepared. Got a pen? I'll give you directions where to meet me."

"Guess I don't have much choice, do I?" asked Pecore in a dull tone.

Before he hung up, Lew made him repeat the directions to be sure he had them right. *An orthopod, huh,* thought Lew as she put her phone away. *Wonder if he's having some surgery? That would explain why he's still sober.* She knew that anyone about to have a knee or hip replacement would be told by some orthopedic surgeons to stay off alcohol for at least two weeks beforehand. Now wouldn't that be just like Pecore—schedule major surgery and not tell her until the last minute?

Turning the squad car around, Lew headed for the entrance to the national forest. She had been relieved to find the man fairly articulate, but then the day was young. Because her mind kept wandering back to the events of the morning, she found she had to check the directions from Dani twice. Even so she still managed to miss the side road leading back to where she needed to be. Frustrated, she willed herself to concentrate on the dire task ahead. Nevertheless, she knew the grave concern on Doc's face would haunt her morning.

• • •

It had been three years since Lewellyn Ferris and Dr. Paul Osborne met unexpectedly on a riverbank one quiet June evening. Lew was there because the owner of Ralph's Sporting Goods had hired her to teach one of his customers how to cast a fly rod. Not yet promoted to chief, she had the time and jumped at the chance to moonlight teaching the sport she loved.

She assumed the customer would be similar to others Ralph had sent her way: a young doctor, college professor, or engineer—the classic young professional—new to the Northwoods, home of the largest population of native brook trout in the country. But to her surprise the student she was expecting was not the usual young professional but her dentist! At least he *had been* her dentist. It was two years since Osborne had retired from his practice.

She learned later that her new student had been just as surprised. He had been told to meet "Lou"—whom he assumed was a guy—for a lesson in casting a fly rod. Not just any fly rod but one that he had purchased years earlier and never used for a rather sad reason, as Lew would discover as she got to know Osborne better.

Over the months that Lew and Osborne spent time together in the water—thanks to his interest in having her teach him how to cast and to a personal chemistry that surprised them both—she could tell that Mary Lee, his late wife, had not been a woman naturally given to kindness. Nor was she appreciative of the time her husband might need to refuel from long hours in the dental office by spending time on the water fishing alone or with other fishermen.

From the snippets of information that escaped from Osborne during moments when he let down his guard while wading in the trout stream, Lew was able to piece together an understanding of his life as a husband and a father and a man who had loved the outdoors since childhood. That was when she learned the history behind his showing up for his first lesson with the fly rod. Even though he was a longtime muskie fisherman, Osborne said he had been so intrigued by the stories of friends touting the thrills of fishing "the shark of the north" that he had decided to give it a try and bought himself a fly rod.

"Problem was," he told Lew, "I forgot to ask permission."

Once Mary Lee got wind of the $300 purchase, she had ranted for days. "What? You already fish two days a week. Look at all the money spent on those dumb fishing lures and muskie rods. Paul, I need a new sofa—not a fishing rod!" Osborne had shared that story in a tone of embarrassment as if he had made a mistake and should have known better.

To appease his wife, he had hidden the rod away without ever attaching a reel or threading the fly line. But with Mary Lee now "redecorating the big house in the sky" (as his neighbor, Ray Pradt, liked to say) he was free to give fly-fishing a try.

Lew, on hearing of Mary Lee's reaction to her husband's interest in learning something new and exciting (to him), was happy she would never have to meet the woman. She also found herself admiring Osborne's loyalty to a wife who did not (in Lew's opinion) deserve it.

That first night of instruction three years ago went so well that Osborne asked if he could have another lesson . . . and another. As the lessons multiplied, Lew could see that Osborne might be a man of a certain age but young at heart with an enthusiasm for spending time in the trout stream that matched hers.

During the first winter that she had known him, she taught him how to tie trout flies. A man who had loved the field of dentistry where he worked with agile fingers in a small space, Osborne delighted in the art of tying trout flies and was happy to find a new hobby in his retirement. Before long, he had decided to rename a seldom-used space in his house (his late wife's beloved formal dining room) and called it the "dead animal room," filling it with all the tools and accessories needed for tying trout flies: more feathers and moose manes, squirrel tails and hunks of deer hair than he could use in a lifetime. The nights that Lew chose to bring her equipment and tie beside him were the best. After an hour or more of fly tying, they would retire to sit in front of the log fire burning in his living room. Fine evenings that ended well.

During these hours Lew learned that although Osborne might be retired from his dental practice, he had never left the science, especially his interest in forensic odontology with which he'd had experience when he was in the military. Because forensic dentistry remains the gold standard for identifying dead bodies, Lew was delighted to discover she might have an alternative to the dreaded Pecore.

And so it was that Osborne found himself deputized so often he began to think of helping out the Loon Lake Police Department as his second career. It did not hurt that the position of deputy coroner kept him close to his fly-fishing instructor.

• • •

Lew drove her squad car onto a grassy area alongside the road where two forest rangers and Pecore were waiting. Behind the three men, she could see a hint of a path, likely a deer trail, leading into the woods.

"I asked the kayakers who found the body to stay at the site," said one of the rangers as she approached. "I wasn't sure if you and Mr. Pecore could find us if we didn't wait for you out here. It's about a half-mile trek to get back there—think you can make it?" As he spoke, he gave Pecore a worried glance. A skinny, small-boned man with a face wizened by weather and booze, Pecore had walked with a limp ever since Lew had known him. The half-mile trek might be a challenge.

"I'll give it a try but I'm scheduled for a hip replacement later this week," said Pecore, "might need a hand if it's rocky or steep." He looked at Lew and said, "How 'bout you take some photos and I wait here?"

"Good try, Pecore, but I'm afraid that's not legal," said Lew in a dry tone. She didn't add that she knew he knew better. How many times had he been chastised by the Wausau Crime Lab for his sloppy work? She shook her head and the forest rangers motioned for them to follow. Against her better wishes, Lew decided to walk behind Pecore in case he fell.

Chapter Five

After pausing three times to let Pecore catch his breath, they arrived at the Pine River where a man and woman in shorts and T-shirts stood, waiting. Two dark green kayaks had been pulled onto a hillock of swamp grass behind them.

As Lew approached, walking ahead of the rangers and Pecore, the woman pointed to a spot twenty feet away. A once-vivid neon green-and-black snowmobile suit bobbed in the gentle rhythm of the slow-moving current.

"Everyone, please stay back," said Lew, scanning the riverbank for footprints. She was hoping to see that very little had been disturbed in the area surrounding the body. "I want one path up to and back from the victim with only two of us examining the body—myself and Mr. Pecore, the Loon Lake coroner. Mr. Pecore," she waved Pecore forward, "would you examine the remains while I get details from the witnesses, please?"

After writing down the couple's names and address, she asked them how they had discovered the corpse.

"Pretty simple," said the man, "just paddling through here and watching for loon nests when we spotted it. I work for the DOT in Rhinelander so I called into our office and asked them to call 911. I knew the back road we took to where we put in but it isn't well marked. I was hoping the office could pinpoint our location here through the GPS on my phone. Easier than asking a 911 operator to guess. I hope I did the right thing."

"You did fine," said Lew, watching as Pecore leaned over the body, which was lying face down. "Hey, before you touch anything," said Lew, dashing over to grab Pecore by the arm, "put these on—on the off chance this isn't an accident. Please, Pecore, it only takes two seconds to be careful. Recently I've had too many families question circumstances and demand autopsies. And autopsies cost a lot of money so let's be sure." What she didn't mention was the way the Wausau boys from the crime lab rolled their eyes every time they had to deal with Pecore's shoddy reports and sloppiness in the vicinity of crime scenes. She handed him a pair of Nitrile gloves. "No unnecessary moving of that body and no fingerprints."

"Oh gosh—you really think someone might have killed this person?" asked the woman. "We've been thinking whoever it is must have gone through the ice by accident."

"Very likely that is what happened," said Lew, "but just in case . . ."

Pecore yanked the sterile gloves from her and pulled them on. "I really don't think this is necessary, Ferris," he said, deliberately dropping her title, "but you're in charge."

"Yes, I am," said Lew, staring down as Pecore prodded at the remains enough to determine the obvious: The snowmobiler was dead, the remains skeletal.

"You know, Chief Ferris," said one of the rangers also watching Pecore's movements, "if that snowmobile suit had not snagged on a sunken log running along the bank there, we might have been out of luck finding the victim. Those suits weigh a lot when they're dry. Waterlogged I'll bet they have to be heavy as rocks, enough to keep a body anchored on the river bottom.

"The Pine is only eight feet deep at its deepest—but, hell, that's deep enough to hide a body." He looked at the couple. "We're lucky you two came kayaking down this way. Summers not too many people use the Pine River—it's slow and buggy. But winter it freezes early and can be a speedway for snowmobilers—*if* you know how to find it."

"You can see the snowmobile submerged over there," said the woman, pointing toward the middle of the river. "It's pretty close to the surface and the water is so clear you can see the key in the ignition."

"My opinion? He drowned," said Pecore getting to his feet. He pulled off the Nitrile gloves and thrust them into the pocket of his dirty blue windbreaker. "Chief Ferris, you give me the paperwork later and I'll fill in the death certificate."

"Whoa, how can you say that?" asked one of the rangers. "Look at the skull—the right side is half blown away. I don't think it's a drowning."

"I agree with my colleague," said the second ranger who had been quiet since they arrived. "If we had rocks where the body might have been pushed around by a current, maybe, but this is all swamp grass and tag alders along here."

"Animals," said Pecore, challenging anyone to argue. "Predator activity. That's what happens when people die outdoors."

"Coyotes don't swim," said one ranger.

"Neither do wolves," said the other. "At least I don't think so."

"Bears," said Pecore. "One swat from a bear can do that."

"Pecore, please, don't overreach your capabilities," said Lew. "All I need from you is the official determination that the victim is deceased. Period."

"Okay, forget I said he drowned," said Pecore with a shrug of his shoulders.

After pulling on a new pair of Nitrile gloves, Lew knelt to roll the figure over. Time, water, and weather had worked on the remains so there was no odor. She unzipped the front of the snowmobile suit and felt for an interior pocket. Her fingers touched a wallet. She pulled it out and opened it. In it was a laminated driver's license. Lew got to her feet.

"Mr. Pecore," she said. "I got news for you."

Pecore snorted. "Yeah?"

"We have to get the Wausau boys out here ASAP."

"Oh, for chrissake." Pecore threw his hands up in disgust. "Do you know how long that will take? I have medical appointments later today and first thing tomorrow. I can't be standing out here all day. Chief Ferris, you are making a mountain out of a simple snowmobile accident."

Lew shrugged. "Maybe."

She turned to the rangers and the two kayakers. Holding out the license, she said, "I am familiar with the name of this victim. He has been on the missing person's list since February." As she spoke, jaws dropped in unison. "The name is Peter Corbin and he is—was—a banker from Wausau. The family has been searching for him since he told them he was planning to stay with friends at a deer shack up near Eagle River. He never arrived." She looked down at the body. "I wonder how he got way the heck out here?"

"I tell you, he fell through a break in the ice and drowned," said Pecore, fuming. "Just because he has been missing does not prove foul play."

"We'll see," said Lew. "Meanwhile, you stay with the body until the Wausau boys get here."

"Me?" Pecore looked like he would have a heart attack. "I don't have time. Later today I'm supposed to check in at the clinic for tests before my hip replacement. I can't stay here."

"I'll tell the boys at the crime lab they need to hurry," said Lew with an understanding smile. "Oh, and by the way, Pecore, nice of you to let me know beforehand that you'll be on medical leave for what—six weeks or more?"

"I was going to let you know when I knew exactly what time," Pecore mumbled.

"Is it okay for us to leave?" asked the woman kayaker, obviously eager to avoid listening to an unpleasant exchange.

"Sure," said Lew, "but please back away from this area carefully. "This may be a crime scene." She watched as the two maneuvered their kayaks back into the river.

As they passed near the submerged snowmobile, the woman gave a yelp. "I see what looks like a helmet down there! It's dark and kind of round."

One of the rangers took off his shoes, rolled up his pant legs, and waded into the shallows. Lew handed him a long branch that she found on the bank. Holding the branch out in front, he was able to snag a strap on the dark object.

"Be careful not to touch it," said Lew as the ranger sloshed his way to the riverbank, the helmet dangling from the branch. "We'll carry it back to my cruiser. I have evidence bags in the trunk."

She examined the helmet hanging in front of her. The strap was in good condition, hooked to what remained of the right side of the helmet, which was covered with nicks.

"Reminds me of a Kevlar helmet I use for target practice," said one of the rangers, "*after* I shoot it."

"Pecore, I heartily recommend you record 'cause of death unknown' when you do the paperwork later. No bear did this."

"Are you calling Wausau now or later?" said Pecore, shoulders drooping as he looked for a spot to sit down.

"I'll take care of it," said Lew. She started toward the woods with the rangers behind her. She paused and turned back to Pecore. "Don't worry, I'll have Officer Donovan relieve you within the hour."

Chapter Six

"Erin, Mark, I'll be down in the waiting room if you need a break," said Osborne. The three of them were standing in the hall outside the isolation ward where Cody had just been moved to keep him from exposing any of the other children in the hospital. While they waited, a team of nurses and doctors buzzed around setting up a dizzying array of medical devices. At the center of all the activity lay Cody—sound asleep.

"He's sedated," said one of the nurses in response to a questioning glance from Mark. "Right now his vitals are okay. Someone on the nursing staff will be here at his bedside around the clock until we know more. Immediate family members are welcome to stay, too. But we ask that everyone wear the disposable masks and gowns that are in that box outside the room. Just a precaution."

"Erin and Mark, you stay here with the nurse," said Osborne. "I'll wait outside in case you need a break but there isn't enough room for all of us."

"Thanks, Dad," said Erin, giving him a hug. She checked her watch. "Dr. Schrieber said the infectious disease specialist should be here shortly. I'll come get you after we talk to him. One of us needs to go check on Beth and Mason."

"Fine," said Osborne. "I'm not leaving until we hear the test results and if you need me to stay the night, just say so."

Tears in her eyes, Erin squeezed his hand.

Osborne headed for the emergency room waiting area. As he rounded the corner, he realized there would be no way he could avoid talking to Bud Jarvison now. With an internal sigh of exasperation, he prepared himself to deal with the man who had been a pain in the neck since they were kids.

During their teens, when Osborne was home from Jesuit boarding school, he found himself competing with Bud for the same girls. Bud, the six-foot-four football hero with the teasing blue eyes. Bud, the lucky kid whose sixteenth birthday gift was a zippy blue Pontiac convertible. Rare was the girl who could resist.

After college and two years into running one of his family's twelve banks, the *Milwaukee Sentinel* newspaper declared Bud Jarvison "Wisconsin's Bachelor of The Year." The advent of branch banking had turned the sleepy small-town Jarvison family banking operation into a multimillion-dollar corporation.

After his father died, Bud sold the company for $30 million, keeping only the position of chairman of the board and a hefty salary. Bud Jarvison had it all: prestige, charisma, and cash.

But although he might be one of the most prominent people in the Loon Lake region, Osborne knew him as a man who lingered too long when a wounded deer needed another bullet, a man legendary for his prowess at cheating on his wife. The year he told the fellas at the deer shack that he had "bagged" over a thousand women *since his marriage* was the last year Osborne hunted with that crowd.

Nor did it help that Bud and his wife, Nancy, found paying their dental bills beneath them. At the time Osborne sold his practice, the Jarvisons owed him thousands of dollars. He wrote it off.

And now he had to share the waiting room with the jerk? Jeez Louise. How bad can one day get?

But Bud was nowhere in sight when Osborne entered the waiting room. Relieved, he picked up an issue of *Consumer Reports* hoping reviews of electric hand drills would take his mind off his grandson and the menace of meningitis. He hadn't turned two pages when a bear paw grabbed his shoulder.

"Chrissstopher," said Bud Jarvison, his voice whistling through the empty waiting room as he exaggerated the first syllable of his late son's name.

Concerned over what was coming next, Osborne braced himself.

"I have been there, Doc. I know just how you must be feeling."

No, you don't, thought Osborne, flinching as Bud plunked himself down beside him and, propping his elbows on his knees, shoved his florid face so close Osborne could not avoid looking into his eyes.

"Worried to death you gotta be. I was down in Nancy's room and overheard the nurses talking. My God, I want you to know if there is *anything*—"

"Why is Nancy here?" asked Osborne, desperate to change the subject.

"Orthopedic surgery. She fell walking the dogs and they've had to rebuild her left shoulder—too much golf didn't help either. She'll be fine," said Bud with a dismissive wave. "Fifteen years since we lost Christopher—do you believe it's been that long?"

Helpless, Osborne shook his head.

"Christopher . . ." Bud repeated the name, his tone softer. "You know, his mother insisted I call him 'Christopher.' No 'Chris.' No 'Topher,' no 'Bud, Jr.' No sirree—had to be 'Christopher.' She hasn't forgiven me, you know. Every time she has more than one martini, she starts." Bud raised his voice to a whine as he mimicked his wife. "'All your fault, Bud. You're the idiot who *had* to buy him that goddamn stupid—etcetera, etcetera.' But what the hell, Doc, you know how she is."

Did Osborne ever. The mere thought of Nancy jarred another childhood memory: Bud's parents. His father had been a genial man who wore an expression of perpetual surprise on his face as if astounded at being the beneficiary of three generations of bankers and inheriting millions without lifting so much as a golf club.

Miriam Jarvison, the family matriarch, was as cool as her husband was friendly. As a young boy, Osborne had been fascinated by the sight of the tall, thin woman with milk-white skin and shiny black hair pulled tight into a bun at the back of her neck. Mrs. Jarvison, Sr. never missed Sunday Mass. A haughty presence always in the same pew, always alone, and always wearing an ankle-length mink coat except in the heat of the summer when the coat was replaced with a rope of beady-eyed minks, their teeth biting their tails to protect her queenly shoulders. The young, motherless Osborne had envied Bud. What must it be like to be loved by such an aloof and lovely woman?

It wasn't until his teen years that he realized it might not have been fun. Though her only child was a boy, Miriam Jarvison made it clear to Bud and his young pals that she considered boys to be smelly, dirty, and not welcome in her mansion where plastic runners covered the expensive rugs.

Osborne's father liked to joke, "Miriam's got a smile sure to terrify a young child." But on the few occasions that Osborne saw her up close it was the woman's eyes that scared him: black and ice cold.

When Bud married Nancy Binghamton, the debutante daughter of an auto executive from Grosse Pointe, Osborne assumed Bud had fallen in love with a woman quite unlike his mother. Tall, blond, and athletic, Nancy Jarvison was as imposing as her husband—and a bully.

Osborne learned that firsthand when Mary Lee, his late wife, found herself banished from the bridge table *and* the Loon Lake Garden Club. All because Nancy perceived Mary Lee as paying too much attention to Bud during cocktails at the Loon Lake Café before a fish fry one Friday night.

Because Bud's reputation as a philanderer was well known, Osborne had assumed his wife was not guilty until the day he overheard her counseling Mallory, their eldest daughter, "to be sure to marry a man like Mr. Jarvison who can buy you nice things."

So Nancy may have been right: A shark may have been circling. Mary Lee never hid her disappointment that Osborne had chosen to take over his father's dental practice in "backwoods Loon Lake" instead of moving to Milwaukee or Minneapolis where "you can make a lot more money, Paul."

If Nancy was a good golfer, she was even better at holding a grudge. Mary Lee Osborne was banned from Loon Lake society for two years. Two years of crying herself to sleep after berating Osborne for having done "something" to cause her banishment. Two years during which Osborne made sure that whenever there was a social event to which they were not invited, he went fishing. It gave Mary Lee an excuse for their absence and he got shelter from the storm.

Then something unexpected happened. Osborne's daughter Erin was assigned to the same second grade class as Christopher Jarvison. Reading and math came easy to Erin, but Christopher struggled.

One day, clueless to the tension between the two mothers, the second grade teacher suggested Erin help Christopher with his math and reading assignments. When Nancy balked, the teacher said in a firm voice, "Erin Osborne is a sweet and friendly little girl. She'll make it easy for your son. He won't be embarrassed to try."

Nancy approached Mary Lee warily only to have Mary Lee pretend that nothing had ever happened between them and agree to whatever play dates might work for Nancy. Whew! Soon she was back at the bridge table, back in the garden club.

Ten years later disaster hit the Jarvison family. For his high school graduation, Bud bought Christopher a bright red ROV, a custom-made recreational off-road vehicle with four-wheel-drive and dual bucket seating. That same week, after a night of partying with beer and single malt Scotch whisky stolen from his parents' bar, Christopher took a girl out for a ride.

Driving down a steep embankment five miles out of town, the ROV rolled over, pinning Christopher and slicing his femoral artery. The girl panicked and ran home. She told no one about the accident until the next morning when Nancy started calling Christopher's friends because he wasn't answering his cell phone. He had bled out.

"Thanks for your concern, Bud," said Osborne. "I remember your loss but I'm sure you'll understand this is hard for me to discuss right now."

Bud reached over to pat Osborne's knee. "Of course. Was it Chief Ferris who found your grandson?"

"Gosh, no," said Osborne. "I brought him in. Since I started helping out as coroner when Pecore isn't available, Chief Ferris has become a family friend. She stopped by to see if she could help."

"Oh?" asked Bud. He paused as if expecting Osborne to say more.

"Dad," said Erin, walking into the waiting room. "Can we talk for a minute?"

"If you'll excuse me," said Osborne to Bud as he jumped to his feet.

• • •

Bud watched Osborne leave the room, his eyes thoughtful. He decided to increase his visits to his wife over the next few days. He would like to know more about Doc's "family friend."

The days when he could call one of the Loon Lake police officers for information on people of interest to him had ended when the Ferris woman became chief of the Loon Lake Police Department. Was this a chance to get back in the loop?

Chapter Seven

As Osborne drove home, he reflected on how the death of a child can change a marriage. When it came to the Jarvisons, it struck Osborne that the loss of Christopher seemed to drain all that was good from that relationship. A certain sourness tainted it from then on. Nancy grew more strident while Bud skirted the edge of boorishness.

Nancy moved on from bullying the women in her bridge club and the Loon Lake Garden Club to engage in ruthless maneuvering to become president or chairperson of every organization that hinted of prestige: the county library, the hospital, one of the Jarvison banks—even the Loon Lake Food Pantry. It was obvious to Osborne that she chose to fill the hole in her heart with people, people, people.

In his way, Bud did the same though he retired from day-to-day management of the new bank-holding company. As chairman, he attended the board meetings but those were sandwiched between full days on the golf course, more hours at the rifle range, fishing trips to Canada, and at least six weeks at deer camp for both bow and rifle seasons.

The few times the Jarvisons appeared together at social events or joined other couples for Friday fish fry they seemed determined to avoid each other. Osborne commented to his late wife that he would see them sit across from one another, turn their gazes in opposite directions, and never say a word to each other across the table.

Within a year of Christopher's death Nancy changed her style, too. From a woman who had always worn what Mary Lee called "tailored clothes," she began to dress more seductively. It was no secret that she worked out with a personal trainer almost every day, which led Osborne to theorize she was simply trying to capitalize on her own good health. That was until one fateful day in his office.

Nancy was in the dental chair for a final polishing of a crown that he had made for her when he happened to glance down and see that the white paper bib pinned to protect her clothing had slipped to one side. The shirt below had been left unbuttoned to expose the landscape of her torso from neck to navel. Osborne was so stunned that for a long moment he sat without moving. Unsure as to whether or not the bib had been deliberately positioned, he gave a nod to his dental assistant and the two of them excused themselves from the room.

"Do you see that?" he asked the young woman assisting him.

"I sure do. I'm assuming you got us out here to give her a few minutes to rearrange herself, Dr. Osborne."

"That is exactly why we are here," said Osborne. "Now if we go back and that bib is not back where it belongs—"

"I'll take care of it," said the assistant.

"Thank you. You'll save me the embarrassment. I'm sure it's an accident."

"Really?" From her expression on her face, it was obvious his dental assistant didn't think there was anything accidental about it at all.

Back at the chair, Osborne was relieved to see that Nancy's bib had been slightly readjusted. He refused to check the buttons on the blouse, hoping that as he reached for an instrument his assistant would be wise enough to straighten the napkin further—which she did with a wink in his direction.

Later that afternoon, Osborne puzzled over the woman's behavior. What on earth could she possibly want from him? Surely Bud Jarvison was a better provider and always would be. They were a handsome couple, too.

What became clear over the years after Christopher's death was that Nancy Jarvison excelled at holding a grudge. In fact Mary Lee may have been one of few women to regain her friendship once Nancy had decided to shut her out of Loon Lake's social circles. And even though she protected her ownership of her husband, she made it a habit to snipe at the man she blamed for her son's death. Over the years, the rancor between the two escalated to a point that even Osborne's McDonald's coffee buddies would comment on how uncomfortable it was to be in a gathering where the two Jarvisons were together.

But if Bud took the abuse in public, he got his revenge: the drinking, the flagrant womanizing, and snide putdowns of his wife when she wasn't around.

When it came to understanding why those two stayed together, Osborne felt the most telling moment may have been Bud's joke on the last night that Osborne spent at deer camp with the guys.

"What's the one surefire way to lose most of your money?" Bud had asked the group while puffing on a cigar.

"Gambling?"

"The stock market?"

"Build a shopping mall?" All were suggestions offered by the other hunters.

"No, oh no," said Bud. "Divorce."

Chapter Eight

"The tests show Cody's meningitis is viral, Dad."

"I hope that's good news," said Osborne, putting an arm around his daughter's shoulders. She had calmed down but her voice was shaky.

"Not sure. It means no antibiotics but the most the medical staff can do is try to keep him stable. The specialist . . ." her voice trembled and Osborne drew her closer. Erin took a deep breath and said, ". . . um, the infectious disease guy said they can't tell if he'll make it or not." She pursed her lips, determined not to break down. "Could take days before they'll know . . . Dad?" She buried her head against his chest and sobbed softly. After a moment, she pushed away and wiped at her face. "This doesn't help, does it?"

Erin tried a smile and Osborne gently tugged at the long, blond braid falling over her right shoulder.

"Is there anything I can do?" he asked, feeling helpless.

"How about you go home and take care of things so you can come back later. Mark and I are staying here for now. I talked to Beth. She's got Mason with her so they're okay. Then if you will come back at six, we'll leave and take the girls to get a bite to eat. I'll be back by eight and stay the night. They're putting a cot in Cody's room. Is that okay?"

"Whatever works for you and Mark is fine. Call my cell if anything changes. Love you, sweetie. I'll let Father John know, too—ask him to say some prayers."

With Erin's plan in mind, Osborne headed home to feed the dog. Mike was a well-behaved black lab but he did get hungry. Pulling into his driveway, Osborne glanced down through the stand of red pine bordering his property. He was startled to see one of the Loon Lake Police squad cars parked in front of his neighbor's house trailer. Too bad, he was under the impression Ray Pradt had been on good behavior lately.

Curious to know what was up, Osborne hurried to set out fresh water and food for Mike before scurrying through the trees to Ray's place. Although an average person might be branded a busybody, Osborne's status as a deputy coroner made it okay. He might be on call when Pecore was "disabled" so he qualified as staff.

Approaching the trailer from the rear, he could hear the murmur of voices—one was female. Had to be Lew.

Though the early afternoon sun was high with a light breeze from the west, no one was outside. That was unusual. For the last two summers Ray had preferred to let his dock double as his office. One of his guiding clients had contributed a patio umbrella so he could work there in bad weather unless the temperature dipped below forty. Today it was eighty-two. Something was up.

"Anybody home?" asked Osborne as he pulled open the screen door that doubled as the mouth of a lurid green muskie that had been painted on the outside of the house trailer. Ray and Lew looked up from where they were leaning over a *Wisconsin Gazetteer* map open to a two-page spread on the table.

For an instant Lew smiled as if the sun had just come out and she was basking in it. Those eyes, that smile always tugged at Osborne's heart. Then her eyes darkened as she asked, "How's Cody?"

"Yeah, Doc," said Ray, straightening up and turning toward him. "Chief Ferris just told me about little Cody. How's the kid doin'?"

"We don't know yet," said Osborne. "The good news is he doesn't have a bacterial infection but the doctors said they won't know for days how bad the virus is. Erin sent me home so I could take care of the dog—"

"Doc, just call. I'll see that Mike's okay," said Ray.

"Thanks. I might do that—have to go back to the hospital later. What's happening here?" He looked at Lew.

"Two kayakers found a skeleton in a snowmobile suit half-submerged in the Pine River. Pecore and I drove to the site and, sure enough—it's the remains of a Wausau man who's been missing since February. The snowmobile he was riding is at the bottom of the river. I've got the Wausau boys out there now.

"Curious to know where he might have accessed the river since it is not marked as one of the county's official snowmobile trails. I thought Ray might know someone familiar with the area. It's all national forest back in there—pretty remote."

"I might . . ." Ray paused to study the ceiling above the kitchen table. "Just might . . ." He nodded up and down. ". . . know a woman . . ." Again he paused, deploying a speech pattern of random starts and stops guaranteed to drive most listeners nuts.

People who knew Ray Pradt learned to be patient. They might be held hostage for the moment but they also knew that the thirty-two-year-old fishing and hunting guide was familiar with the Northwoods from the inside out.

When Osborne's buddies gathered 'round for their early morning coffees at McDonald's, they would nod their heads in solemn agreement that whatever his ethical failings, "Ray Pradt's got the eye of an eagle and the ear of an owl. Desperate to find your wounded deer? Call Ray: He can track through twigs."

Further, given a history of misdemeanors he attributed to "youthful discretions (no, that word is not misspelled)," Ray had spent enough nights in the Loon Lake hoosegow that he had earned the respect of folk familiar with the perpetrators, places, and events occurring beyond the purview of most law-abiding Loon Lake residents.

More than once Chief Lewellyn Ferris had confided in Osborne that she valued Ray's tracking skills as much as his access to the bad actors in the region.

And so Osborne pulled out a kitchen chair to sit while he and Lew waited for Ray to finish his thought. After a long moment, Ray said, "Let me . . . make a call. Something . . ." he stared up at the light fixture over the table as if the answer might be dangling there, "does come to mind." Punching buttons on his cell phone, he stood up and headed toward the door. "You two wait here."

"Do we look anxious to leave?" asked Lew, giving him the dim eye. "Just make the damn call, would you please?"

After the screen door banged closed behind Ray, Osborne asked Lew, "Were you referring to that banker who disappeared from his deer camp? Wasn't he running one of the Jarvison banks? You know, I saw Bud this morning. I wonder if he's heard about this?"

"I doubt it," said Lew. "We haven't released any information to the media, though who knows what Pecore has said to anyone. That guy never keeps his trap shut." She rolled her eyes in frustration. "Oh, by the way, numbnut is having a hip replacement this week."

"Oh, for heaven's sake's. Did you just find out today?"

Lew nodded. "Watch. The minute he goes under anesthetic, I'll have a dozen people pass away."

"If that happens, call me."

"You've got your family to worry about."

"True—but I need something to take my mind off a situation about which I can do nothing. Helping you with a death certificate or calling for an autopsy will allow me to do something productive. But, Lew, back to that banker—was it Peter Corbin's remains?"

"Yes. How did you know that?"

"I remember hearing that he was missing and the news stuck with me because he grew up in Loon Lake. The Corbins were patients of my father's."

Osborne got up to pour himself a cup of coffee, and then sat down again. "So what do you think happened? Had he been drinking and ran his sled over bad ice? We must have a dozen of those every winter. Most riders are able to scramble out of the water. Hypothermic but alive."

"That's what I don't know," said Lew. "Pecore tried to say the victim drowned but it looks to me—and I could be wrong—like he may have been shot. The helmet was badly damaged. Half the skull is missing. Pecore argued that critters or current could have the same effect. That's why I called in the Wausau boys."

"That old man running the show give you trouble?"

Lew grinned. "Not this time. I outsmarted him."

More than once Osborne had witnessed Lew's struggles with the head of the Wausau Crime Lab. Fred Boettcher was in his late sixties and, being old school, of the opinion women did not belong in law enforcement: "Certainly not in *my* jurisdiction."

Determined to make the life of Loon Lake Police Chief Lewellyn Ferris difficult, he instituted a two-stage torture template. Initially, he had accused her of overreacting to a potential crime scene saying, "Come on, Ferris, we see bullet holes through the skull all the time: *It's a suicide for chrissake.*"

The first time he tried that, Lew persisted and an autopsy proved her right. The entry wound was at the back of the skull, which made it highly unlikely it was self-inflicted.

Undaunted, Fred then forced her to complete hours of unnecessary paperwork before he would grudgingly assign one of his investigators. That such a delay could compromise a crime scene didn't bother Fred.

After suffering through that process several times—and discovering she was the only law enforcement professional who was required to complete the bogus requests—Lew learned to e-mail her tormentor that the paperwork was "in process," then contact Bruce Peters directly.

Bruce was in his late twenties, well versed in the forensic sciences, and new to fly-fishing—so new that he was fanatic. Once he discovered that Chief Ferris was an expert in the trout stream, he jumped at every chance to work with her.

Lew knew the drill. Every time they worked together, she made sure he got time in the stream. "Bruce, stop muscling that fly line. A good cast is all about *touch*—not strength. Try it again."

And so Lew had learned to alert Bruce when she needed help—and let him finagle the assignment to a Loon Lake Police investigation. Fred had no clue.

"Today was my lucky day, Doc. I got Bruce on the phone right away. He jumped in his car and he's at the site now. He called in two scuba divers to help search the river bottom—"

Before she could say more, Ray banged through the screen door. "Okay, I got hold of Sherry. She and her husband are home today and I told her we'd be right over—"

"Who's Sherry?" Lew interrupted.

"An old girlfriend," said Ray. "She married Russell Kelliher and they raise Plott hounds for bear hunters. She said the DNR has declared a four-mile buffer zone along that stretch of the Pine River—right where you said that body was found. Hunters lost seven hounds to wolves there last winter.

"When I told her that a snowmobile had gone down in the river, she said, 'Makes no sense, Ray. *No one who knows the Pine goes anywhere near that area.*'"

Chapter Nine

The Kellihers' yellow frame house sat high up on a rise from the county road. The land around the house and a small barn behind it had been cleared of trees so the house appeared to be surrounded by gently sloping acres of fresh-mown lawn. The entire property was surrounded with an electric fence that ran close to the drive and right up to the buildings. Half a dozen dogs were lazing about in the pasture.

"I hope someone owns a riding mower," said Lew drily as she drove up the paved driveway. Before she could turn off the ignition a tall, wide-shouldered man with short dark hair and a full beard stepped out onto the front stoop.

Ray jumped out of the backseat saying, "Yo, Russell, hope we aren't keeping you."

"Heck no, you folks come right in," said the man, holding open the door behind him. "Good morning, Chief Ferris, I'm Russell Kelliher and the shy little woman you'll meet in the kitchen is my wife, Sherry—she's a Ray Pradt survivor." He chuckled at his joke while shaking Lew's hand before introducing himself to Osborne.

"Shy, my eye," said a cheery voice from the kitchen just to the right of the front foyer. Sherry Kelliher was a petite blond with short curly hair. Faded jeans and a black tank top showed off her slim, muscled figure. She had lively eyes and a well-tanned face, evidence she spent a lot of time outdoors.

"Sorry I'm so sweaty," she said, "I was just out working a couple of the dogs."

She gave Ray a friendly peck on the cheek before herding the three of them toward the kitchen table where a portable coffeepot and cups sat behind a large map that had been spread out over a blue-and-white checked tablecloth. The kitchen was neat and smelled of dog.

"Help yourselves to coffee," said Sherry. "Russell and I have been worried about the increasing numbers of depredations, which is the term the DNR uses for the killing of dogs by wolves. Why they don't just call them 'dog kills' I don't know. Depredation is an awfully big word."

"Whatever they want to call it, too many fine dogs, trained for hunting bear, are being killed these days—seventeen in the last six weeks," said Russell.

"Seventeen? That many just in this area?" asked Lew. "Are you sure? That's a lot."

"In this multicounty region," said Russell. "I keep track of the packs and I can show you their territories on this map I put together. I made a list of the packs that have killed dogs recently and just listen to the stats I got.

"The Venison Creek Pack killed a four-year-old Plott hound, the Lost Creek Pack a seven-year-old Plott hound, the Ranger Island Pack—their territory is just west of here—got two Plott hounds. The Flag River Pack 'depredated' two redbones in training, the Carps Creek Pack got a three-year-old male redtick, the Crescent Flats Pack went after a German shorthaired pointer, and in the Nicolet National Forest the Black Lake Pack got a Walker hound—"

"Excuse me, Russell, but is this unusual?" asked Lew. "Have wolves always been this aggressive?"

"More wolves, more packs," said Russell. "Now, I'm not saying wolves don't have their place in the food chain but Sherry and

I aren't the only trainers of hounds for bear hunting who are of the opinion that just maybe it's time for more controls over this goddamn wolf population."

"Have any humans been attacked?" asked Osborne.

"Not that we know of . . . yet," said Russell. "When he called, Ray said you got someone maybe lost back in the Nicolet somewhere—that's not good and I'll tell you why."

"I'll cut him off after ten minutes," said Sherry with a smile.

"Here's the deal," said Russell, hitching his chair closer to the table and pouring a fresh cup of coffee. "Sometime in June the packs gather with their newborn pups in what's called a 'rendezvous site.' These sites are used once the pups are weaned and they stay there until the nomadic hunting periods in the fall and winter when they can join the pack.

"So any people or dogs entering a rendezvous site are at risk?" asked Osborne.

"Definitely the dogs. You may be surprised to hear that the value of the dogs lost this year alone had to be $30,000 or $40,000," said Russell. "These are not mutts—these are purebred dogs trained to hunt bear.

"Once the DNR hears about a depredation and the owner can pinpoint the location, then they establish a caution area, usually a four-mile buffer around a depredation site. And that's what's been happening all along the Pine River in the Nicolet National Forest. Like I told Ray, no one is going near there these days. Not for training their dogs, not for hiking, and not for picnics. You got grandchildren? You better find somewhere else to take 'em wading."

"Are you saying that once the hunting periods start in the fall and winter, the rendezvous sites will be safe?"

"We don't know that," said Russell. "Wolf packs are territorial. I don't think it's wise to challenge them in areas where you know they have killed dogs. Who knows what a wolf is thinking?"

"I take it you two are training your hounds elsewhere?" asked Lew.

"Yeah, like in our backyard," said Sherry with a laugh. "No, we've found forest areas where it's safe to train them right now but we are keeping our eyes open. You never know when a new pack might form and establish a territory."

"Wolves are very intelligent," said Russell. "My advice? If you think you'll be searching in that buffer zone along the Pine, then keep your eyes and ears open. Wolves howl to enforce their territory. You hear that—scram."

Chapter Ten

"Can you show us exactly where the danger zone is in the national forest?" asked Ray.

"Sure," said Russell, pulling the map toward him. Lew and Osborne stood up to look over his shoulder. "It starts up here and runs from a logging road south to this section—then figure a four-mile radius around that stretch." With his finger, he drew a circle that showed the Pine River running through its center.

"What makes it even more dangerous for dogs like ours is that this particular rendezvous site is within the territories of three wolf packs. Incidentally, one entire wolf pack area will average forty to sixty square miles. Sherry and I happen to know the trainers who lost four hounds to wolves in or around that rendezvous site since late May. Now everyone knows to avoid the area—bear hunters, bird hunters, deer hunters, everyone."

"I assume it's posted," said Osborne.

Russell shook his head. "No idea. We haven't been back there in ages."

• • •

Half an hour later, Lew pulled into the clearing at Ray's trailer to drop him and Osborne off.

"I'll check with you later, Doc. I have to call Bruce—maybe Pecore is right and it was wolves who got to Corbin after he drowned. There must be a food source around there. If they have been weaned and aren't old enough to hunt, what do you think the pups eat?"

"You mean besides expensive bear hounds?" asked Osborne.

"Small children," said Ray. "Just kidding."

Lew's cell phone rang. As she glanced down at the number on the screen, Osborne and Ray got out of cruiser. "It's the dispatch center," said Lew before Osborne shut the door. "Something must be up. Dani has instructions not to call me unless it's an emergency Officer Donovan can't handle or if it's Bruce checking in. Excuse me while I take this call."

As the screen door to Ray's trailer banged shut behind them, Ray said, "Wait here, Doc. I'll be right back." He walked through the small kitchen and down the narrow hall to his bedroom. A minute later he returned with a book in his hands. Thrusting it at Osborne, he said, "Here, give this to the little guy. Tell him it's my favorite book and when he feels better I'll take him out for muskies."

Osborne looked down at a worn copy of *Lunkers Love Nightcrawlers*. "Gee, Ray, thank you but I'm not sure Cody reads at this level. He's only seven."

"If that's the case, how . . . 'bout . . . you . . ." Ray pointed an index finger at Osborne, "read it to him."

"That's an idea. Good idea. I'll give it a try."

Osborne knew better than to let skepticism dampen his friend's heartfelt intention. He would indeed give *Lunkers* a try. The promise of fishing with Ray would thrill Cody. The youngster adored his grandfather's friend, to the point that at times Osborne felt more than a little jealous of his neighbor.

After a quick flip through the pages of the book, Osborne grinned at Ray who smiled back in silent agreement. Now Cody *had* to get better—not only did he have Ray's favorite book to read but a date to go after muskies!

Holding the screen door open, Lew leaned into the room. "Hey, you two. I'm expecting a visitor any minute—a man from Chicago who called the dispatch center early this morning. Said he was driving up and asked to meet with me when he got to town. I assumed he would call before he arrived and I'd told Dani to forward the call if I wasn't back. But he was just at the station and she misunderstood my message. She thought I meant for her to 'forward' him so he's on his way out here."

"Anything serious?" asked Osborne.

"Not sure. Worried about his son. Apparently the kid is a college student, a summer intern, and has gone missing from the Bass Lake Natural Resources Center. The folks at the center aren't too worried—students have a habit of going camping and forgetting to tell the office staff that they'll be gone for a few days. But this boy's father is pretty upset."

"Sounds like a good time for me to head home," said Osborne, getting to his feet.

"And I have a ton of gear I need to set up for three clients I'm taking on the Rainbow Flowage tonight," said Ray.

"Too late," said Lew, her eyebrows raised in apology at the sound of tires outside the trailer.

A black Lincoln Navigator had pulled up behind Lew's cruiser. A tall man dressed for a day at the office got out of the car and looked around. Without saying a word, he took in the sight of the battered house trailer adorned with the gaping jaws of the lurid green muskie, the gleaming new pontoon tied to the dock and bouncing lightly on the water, Lew in her khaki police uniform walking toward him and, right behind Lew, Osborne in dark slacks and a blue-and-white-check button-down shirt open at the neck. Even at the sight of Ray in camouflage shorts and a bright green T-shirt emblazoned with *Fishing With Ray: Excitement, Romance, and Live Bait*, the visitor still said nothing.

Watching the newcomer in the clearing, Osborne was relieved that Ray had not insisted on wearing his beloved fishing hat—the one with the stuffed trout sewn on top and positioned so that the head and tail stuck out over his ears. He had reached to put it on before leaving the trailer only to catch a stern look from Osborne. Much as Ray hated missing an opportunity to make an unforgettable first impression, Osborne sensed this was not the time.

Their visitor remained silent, his eyes shifting from the trio walking toward him to the lake shimmering in the afternoon sun. He walked over to the picnic bench holding Ray's tackle boxes, sat down, and dropped his head into his hands. His shoulders heaved but there was no sound. Lew threw a look of caution at Osborne and Ray before sitting down beside the man. She waited. No one spoke.

Osborne checked his watch: not time for him to go back to the hospital just yet. With a nod from Lew, he and Ray slid onto the bench on the opposite side of the picnic table.

Raising his head and taking a deep breath, the man said, "I am so sorry." He mopped at his face with a white handkerchief. "I've been driving since three this morning, haven't eaten, haven't slept in two days, and I know something bad has happened to my son. I know it in my gut. I know it in my heart. I can't prove it, I just . . . know it."

Osborne felt a chill. He knew that feeling.

Chapter Eleven

"Lewellyn Ferris. I'm chief of the Loon Lake Police," said Lew, extending a hand to the man sitting next to her. "I'll do my best to help you find your son.

"Appearances aside," she said with a gesture and slight smile in the direction of Ray, "the two gentlemen sitting behind us are deputies of mine and both are very knowledgeable of the Northwoods. My hunch is one or the other will know right where to look for your son."

Lew stood up and, putting a hand on Osborne's shoulder, said, "I'd like you to meet Dr. Paul Osborne. Doc is a retired dentist and he works with the Loon Lake Police and the Wausau Crime Lab when we need an odontologist. That's forensic dentistry," she added as a look of confusion crossed the man's face.

"And Ray Pradt here is a fishing and hunting guide. He knows just about every body of water and logging lane in the region. Or to put it another way," Lew winked at Ray, "for as long as I have known him, Ray has managed to avoid holding a real job. Not to downplay the seriousness of your situation, sir, but I thought you would appreciate knowing who we are."

"And I do," said the man. "I'm Jake Barber, the guy who called you early this morning, Chief Ferris. My son, Liam, is a grad student in behavioral ecology down in Madison. He has been living up here this summer and working on a research grant studying invasive plant species. We've been in touch all along until he disappeared last weekend."

Osborne studied the man as he spoke. Wide-faced with a firm well-shaven jaw, Barber was plain-spoken and direct. Osborne guessed him to be in his late fifties. If it weren't for his office pallor, he might be someone who enjoyed the outdoors—a runner or cyclist perhaps.

"The facts are this," Barber said in the crisp tone of a man used to giving directions. "Liam is twenty-two years old, he's healthy, and he is familiar with the outdoors. We have fished and hunted for years so it's not like he can't take care of himself. I am very worried because I have not heard from him in the last four days and that is highly unusual. I want to emphasize that: *highly unusual*. We're close. Maybe closer than most fathers and sons— we talk every evening." Jake paused before saying, "We lost his mother to cancer five years ago. So . . . we stay close." He gave an apologetic shrug of his shoulders.

"Does he have a girlfriend?" asked Ray. "I've been known to go missing for weeks when—"

"I wish he did. And, believe me, I would know if he did. He's made friends with the other interns but, no, he has not been dating anyone up here."

Jake looked back at Lew. "Chief Ferris, I did some checking before I left home. My son has not used an ATM or his credit cards. I know because I'm on the accounts. His two best friends have not heard from him either—on Facebook or e-mail or texting. And those guys are always in touch so that's odd, too."

"I see," said Lew. She had pulled out her notebook and was taking notes. "Besides his work on the research project, tell me what else your son does. Hike? Swim? Scuba dive? Go camping? Can you think of anything that might motivate him to go somewhere? Does he carry a cell phone?"

"Yes, he has a phone. But I keep getting the signal 'dropped call.'"

"Not unusual up here," said Osborne.

"Doc is right," said Ray. "I have to stand outside my trailer to get a good signal . . . You see people pulled over and standing on their cars? They're not nuts . . . just trying to get a signal from a cell tower."

"Have you asked your service provider to see if they can trace your son's phone?" asked Lew.

"I didn't think I could do that. Aren't there legal hoops to jump through? That would take weeks. At least that's what customer service told me."

"Customer service is wrong," said Lew. "A missing person is not a missing felon—and they are required to execute a trace immediately."

"Oh no," Jake looked stricken. "You mean this could have been done yesterday?"

"Should have been," said Lew. "Give me the information and I'll call. When it's law enforcement, they sit up straight."

"Here's the cell phone number and the name of our service provider," said Jake, handing her a slip of paper.

Lew hit Speed Dial for the Loon Lake Police dispatch center. After giving directions for calling the service provider and Liam Barber's cell number, she said, "If they give you any trouble, Dani, call me right back. Any news from Bruce yet on those remains we found? Okay, if he calls in, let me know ASAP."

Clicking her cell phone off, Lew turned her attention back to Jake Barber. "Sorry for the interruption but it's important we get that trace underway."

"Thank you," said Jake, relief on his face. "You asked what my son does. He loves to fly-fish, which is a big reason he was looking forward to his internship up here. I own a cabin in Jackson Hole where we go as often as we can. Also Liam spent last year in Japan teaching English as a second language and the father of one of his students taught him a Japanese fly-fishing technique called tenkara. He's been planning to fish tenkara-style up here—see if it works better in narrow trout streams."

"Really," said Lew. "Did he mention where? The names of any streams, rivers, lakes?"

"Yes, I tried to remember some and wrote them down." Jake pulled a wallet from his pants pocket and took out a slip of paper. "The Prairie River, the Ontonagon, and the Bois Brule. He tried tenkara on the Elvoy and said he had just a great night of fishing."

"All well-known trout streams," said Lew. "I fly-fish so I know."

Jake nodded then said, "Recently he was talking about trying to find a way in to a stream that's well off the beaten path. He had a botany professor who told him about a trout stream that has huge brookies—three and four pounders—because few people know about it."

"Wow," said Lew. "I wonder where the hell that could be. I've never seen a brook trout that big. Have you, Ray?"

Ray shook his head. "Sure he wasn't talking largemouth bass?"

"No. Brook trout."

"Do you have the professor's name and number?" asked Lew. "He might point us in the right direction. My worry is he tried finding a place that's so far off the beaten path that he may have gotten lost. Happens up here too often."

"I'll put my secretary on it," said Barber. "I can tell her who to call at the university. My cell phone is in the car. I'll go get it." He jumped up from the picnic table.

"Hold on a minute," said Lew, grabbing his arm. "A couple more questions first. What about you, Mr. Barber? What do you do and how can I can reach you if I need to?"

"Oh, sorry. I run All Tech, a software company with offices in Chicago and I live in Wilmette, Illinois. Liam is my only child and—what more do you need to know? This isn't about me."

"Of course not, but the parents of missing children forget they may be the target. Are you a wealthy man?"

"If you're thinking Liam may have been kidnapped that doesn't strike me as plausible. I know no one who—"

"I'm sure you don't but I want you to give it some thought. This region has a number of summer camps where celebrities and very wealthy people send their children. We've had more than one instance when—"

Barber waved a hand before she could finish. "I see what you mean. But I've had no phone calls, no strange messages, nothing to hint that anyone even knows I've been worried about Liam."

"Last question," said Lew. "Have you already talked with the county sheriff? Checked to see if they've heard or seen anything?"

"He's next on my list but when I stopped by the Bass Lake office, they told me to start with you. Oh, one more thing: Liam's car is missing. It's a staff vehicle—an old Jeep Wrangler. I've got the license number for it." He rummaged through his wallet for another scrap of paper.

"Hold on for a second, Mr. Barber. I'll check in with the sheriff, see if they know anything." Lew reached for her phone. "Hey, Chief Ferris here. Is Sheriff Moore in? Ask him if he has a minute, please? I have details on a missing person I'd like to run by him." Lew covered her phone and said, "I'm putting this on speaker in case you would like to add something."

"Lewellyn, I heard you found that missing banker," said a relaxed male voice. "Don't know if I have much for you on that case, though I—"

"That's not why I'm calling, Garry." Lew interrupted him. Garry was a talker and right now she didn't want to take the time to humor him. "One of the summer interns working out of the Bass Lake Natural Resources Center here in Loon Lake has been missing for four days. He was researching invasive plant species and the family is concerned that he may have wandered too far into a remote area and gotten lost. We're talking city kid here. Who knows if he has a compass much less knows how to use it?

Know what I mean? His car is missing, too. I was hoping some of your people might have found it or could keep an eye out as they're driving around. We'll cover Loon Lake but who's to say he might not be out in the county somewhere."

"Sure, give me the info. I'll post it for our neighboring counties, too. Say, Lewellyn, whereabouts in the national forest were those remains found?"

"Two kayakers spotted the body floating in the Pine River. The Wausau boys are working the site right now. Why?"

"That's what I thought I'd heard. Tell them to be *veeery* careful. Lost one of my best K-9 search and rescue dogs in that area last spring. Wolves. The Violet Lake Pack."

"Thanks, Garry, you're not the first to mention that. Appreciate the help—and the warning." Her phone off, Lew turned to Barber.

"Where are you staying, Mr. Barber?"

"The Loon Lake Inn. Haven't checked in yet. Please, call me Jake."

"Oh, one more thing," said Lew, pulling the notebook from her back pocket again. "Where has your son been living?"

"Liam is sharing an apartment with another intern. Phil Branch is the boy's name. They rented a house near the Loon Lake Library and I've been calling the house phone number but no one answers. I have the address in my car. I went by there the minute I got into town but no one was home."

"You didn't go in?" asked Lew.

"I don't have a key and—"

"Sure, that's understandable," said Lew. "I'd like you to do two things right now. First, make that call to your secretary so we can locate that professor who may know where your son has been fishing. Then follow me into town. We need to check the apartment and talk to Liam's roommate. He may know something." She checked the time. "If the other intern was working today, he should be home by now. We need to catch him before he goes anywhere."

"So . . . you think I'm right about this?" asked Barber. "You think Liam is lost?"

Lew's eyes met his. "I want you to be wrong. I will do my best to prove you wrong."

But Osborne could see that she was worried.

Chapter Twelve

At the last minute, Osborne decided to follow Lew and the others into Loon Lake. After all, Mike would be fine in the backyard and Ray had offered to feed him later that evening.

Their four cars made an odd caravan driving into the little town: Lew's authoritative Loon Lake police cruiser was followed by Jake Barber's imposing black Navigator. Behind the rear bumper of the Navigator chugged Ray's battered pickup, the late afternoon sun flashing off the leaping walleye its owner had fastened to the rusting hood. Bringing up the rear was an uninteresting dark green Subaru, which looked out of place but the retired dentist at the wheel didn't mind.

After parking on a side street in one of Loon Lake's quiet, tree-lined neighborhoods, Jake pointed in the direction of a small frame house with a one-car garage. They gathered on the sidewalk before trooping up to the front stoop. As they neared the house, Lew led the way. Osborne chose to be last in line. One of his pleasures since meeting Lew had been watching her at work.

Although many women her age lived in bodies that had softened with time, Lew's had gained muscle—though the trim fit of her uniform's khaki shirt did little to obscure the fact she was female. Behind her strode Jake Barber, his tall, squarish frame defined by well-cut dress pants. The late afternoon heat had given him an excuse to remove his coat and tie and unbutton the collar of his white shirt. At the moment, he looked less like a distraught father than a businessman intent on negotiations at the bargaining table.

Behind Jake loped Ray whose appearance belied the serious nature of the house call. Lanky, light-footed, and loose-limbed, his torso appeared to move in three sections with the midriff taking the lead followed by long legs followed by head and shoulders—the latter appearing to make a last minute decision to join the rest of his body. Osborne had learned long ago that Ray's casual appearance was a mask. He might look goofy but the man could be trusted to be as alert as a great blue heron: He would not miss a detail—sight, sound, not even a scent—that could lead them to Jake's missing son.

Lew rapped on the front door and waited. No answer. She knocked again and a muffled male voice hollered, "Hey, you guys, take it easy."

Seconds later a sleepy youth who couldn't have been much over the age of twenty yanked open the door. At the sight of his visitors, he stumbled back in surprise. "Whoa, who are you?"

"Police. Does Liam Barber live here?" asked Lew.

"Yeah but he's not home right now. Why?"

Ignoring the question, Lew turned sideways and, indicating Jake, said, "This is Liam's father and I'm Chief Lewellyn Ferris with the Loon Lake Police. Mr. Barber is very concerned that his son may be lost. The staff at the Bass Lake office wasn't much help, so we're hoping you might know something.

"Oh, and these two gentlemen," she waved toward Ray and Osborne, "may be able to help us locate Liam if necessary. May we come in?"

The boy opened the door wide and let them into a small living room that held an old television on a stand in one corner and a sagging brown sofa strewn with T-shirts, a pair of wrinkled cargo shorts, a scruffy blue wool blanket, and a soiled paper plate holding a slice of dead pizza. Two floor lamps with shades that looked as though they had been stepped on and an old wooden desk holding an open laptop computer completed the room's décor. None of it encouraged Osborne to want to sit down.

"Sorry I didn't hear you at first—I was working on my app," said the boy, pointing toward the computer. "Liam and I have to have 'em done before we go back to school." He leaned back against the desk as he spoke.

"When was the last time you saw Liam?" asked Jake, pushing aside the stuff on the sofa and sitting down. He leaned forward on his elbows, hands clasped between his knees.

The intensity of his gaze caused the boy to gulp before he could answer. "Last Monday," said the boy, clearing his throat. "By the way, you guys, I'm Phil," he said as he threw nervous looks at the four adults crowding the room. "Phil Branch. Um, I think it was Monday . . . yeah." A disoriented expression crossed his face as he struggled to remember.

"Too much weed lately?" asked Ray, his voice teasing.

The kid gave a nervous laugh. "Um, no, not really." Thrusting his shoulders back, he said, "Now I remember. Liam said he was planning to work his square on the grid and squeeze in some fishing when he could. I didn't think about his being gone 'cause he keeps a sleeping bag and a two-man tent in the car and lot of times he stays overnight out there."

"Out where? And what's the grid?" asked Lew.

"Oh, here, I'll show you," said Phil, turning to touch the keyboard on the open laptop. The computer screen lit up. "Liam and I are responsible for finding samples of invasive plant species growing in this section of the Nicolet National Forest." He pointed to a colored section on a map, then zoomed in. "See, here? The section is so big that we decided to break it down into squares on a grid and tackle one square at a time. Otherwise you'd go nuts, you know?"

"You're looking at twenty square miles," said Osborne. "That's a heck of lot of forest land to cover on foot."

"Yeah, we call it 'job security,'" said Phil with an attempt at a laugh. "We don't have to do it all this summer but as much as we can." Moving the cursor, he said, "Liam has been working this section and I'm working over here." He pointed.

Ray peered closely at the map. "Did anyone at the Bass Lake office happen to mention to you two guys that you've been working in a wolf rendezvous site?"

"Oh yeah. They gave us whistles. I haven't seen a wolf yet though. Pretty silly if you ask me."

"So you're saying that my son is working this section?" asked Jake, leaning over Phil's shoulder to point at the screen.

"Right. He told me he was hoping to harvest enough plants that he could take a long enough break one afternoon to hike in a couple miles to fish the Pine River. Figured he would have to bushwhack his way in 'cause no one ever goes there."

"Except the wolves," said Osborne.

"You think?" Phil looked up questioning. "I was told they're afraid of people."

"Yes and no," said Ray. "If they feel threatened—or if one of their pups is threatened—you are not going to stop a wolf by blowing a whistle."

The reality of Ray's statement dawned slowly on Phil's face. "Oh my God," he said, his eyes darting from Ray to Lew and Jake. "You don't think . . ."

"Ray, did you put the *Gazetteer* in the truck?" asked Lew.

"I've got one if you need it," said Osborne before Ray could answer. "Want me to grab it?"

"Doc, you have to be at the hospital in an hour," said Lew, glancing at her watch. "Ray, you're officially deputized to assist me on this search as of right now."

"I want to, Chief, but I promised I would guide these two guys from Milwaukee tonight and—"

"How much are they paying you?" asked Jake. Before Ray could answer, he said, "I'll give you five times your fee. Call 'em and cancel."

"Okedoke."

That was one of the few times Osborne had seen Ray take orders from anyone other than Lewellyn Ferris.

Lew's cell phone rang. She listened and covered the mouthpiece. "It's Dani. They've traced the phone." She waited. "No, are you kidding? Thanks." She clicked her cell phone shut. "The signal from Liam's phone indicates it is here in the house. At this location—where is his bedroom?"

"Around the corner on your right," said Phil.

They hurried to a closed bedroom door and Lew pushed it open. An unmade bed, a small plywood dresser, and two folding chairs heaped with clothes that had been thrown at them. A pair of waders hung from a hook on the wall. Lew lifted a three-ring binder from the top of the dresser and under it found a cell phone. She picked it up and pressed the power button. "Um, out of juice."

"That happens a lot. Liam forgets to plug it in at night. His laptop runs down, too."

Jake shook his head. He walked over to the waders and stood staring at them. "I wonder why he didn't take these."

No one had an answer.

As they left the house, Jake's secretary called his cell phone. She had reached the professor and learned that the trout stream he'd told Liam about was in the Nicolet National Forest: the Pine River. Problem was, he hadn't been there in twenty years and couldn't remember how he'd found it. "One of those twisty back roads—I found it by accident," was all he could offer.

Chapter Thirteen

After the nurse's aide removed her dinner tray, Nancy Jarvison relaxed back against the pillows and opened her iPad. She was halfway into the first chapter of the new book she had just downloaded when she heard a bustling in the hall.

"Sssh," she said as loud as she could. She looked down at the screen but the annoying clatter continued, this time punctuated with snorts and feminine laughter.

"Oh, for Pete's sake," she said to herself. "What's the purpose of a private room if I have to listen to all this nonsense? Idiots."

Bracing her bandaged left shoulder with her right hand, she swung her legs over the side of the bed. Peering through the half-open door into the hallway, she could see the two nurse's aides wheeling a large canvas cart toward the next room. She was about to lambast them both when she heard one say, "That's Bud Jarvison's ex-wife in 324. What a bitch. No wonder he dumped her."

"They're divorced? I didn't know that. I have to tell my sister. She had a fling with him a while back. He's a pretty handsome guy even if he is kinda heavy and, man, that dude has money."

"I think they're divorced. Yeah, I'm sure. After fishing last Saturday night, Jimmie and I stopped into Thunder Bay Bar for a couple beers. Bud was there with a woman. He kept trying to get her to stand up for the pole dance contest but she refused. I heard him promise her a hundred bucks if she'd get up and strip."

"For a hundred bucks? I'd do it."

"Yeah, well, she looked to be six months pregnant so I don't think you would if you were that far along."

Nancy backed away from the door. Bud at that disgusting strip joint with another woman? A *pregnant* woman? She could feel her blood pounding in her ears. How many times had he promised not to embarrass her like that?

The aides were moving down the hall, away from her room, still talking. Nancy edged closer to the crack in the door.

"Who's the girlfriend, anyone we know?"

"Never saw her before. But very pretty. I think she's Hispanic. Maybe one of the waitresses from the Mexican restaurant in Rhinelander? Yep, pretty and pregnant—poor thing. She'll be lucky if she gets anything from Bud. Somebody shoulda told her . . ."

Back at her bedside, Nancy picked up her cell phone and pressed familiar numbers. "Hi, Brenda, would you do me a favor? Pick me up tomorrow morning early—like eight o'clock, please? And don't tell Bud. I'm planning a surprise."

She sank onto the bed, thinking. Then she inhaled sharply and, moving carefully, sat back against the pillows. She needed time to figure this out.

She heard a gentle knock on her door and her husband walked into the room. Nancy put a hand to her forehead. "Bud, honey, do you mind? I have an awful headache. Do you mind if we don't visit right now?"

"Of course not, sweetheart. Say, have you heard anything more about how Doc Osborne's grandson is doing?"

"No. Why would I?" The longer he stood there the angrier she got and she did not want him to see that.

"Earlier today you heard a nurse say the boy is very ill."

"Oh that. No I haven't heard anything. Just go, okay?"

Chapter Fourteen

Arriving at the hospital half an hour before Erin was expecting him, Osborne hustled past the waiting room, hoping not to be seen. One quick glance assured him Bud was nowhere in sight. That was a relief.

He found Erin and Mark sitting beside Cody's bed while a nurse was busy recording data she saw on the myriad of instruments connected to his grandson.

"Any change?" asked Osborne.

"No, Dad. But Cody is so sedated right now that I couldn't tell if there was. One of the residents came in a while ago and asked for permission to run additional blood tests for research he's doing. I told him to go ahead. Can't hurt, right?" She glanced at the nurse for confirmation and got a nod back.

"Okay, Dad, you're on. We'll be back in an hour or so."

Osborne sat down in one of their chairs and opened *Lunkers Love Nightcrawlers*. He scooted the chair closer to where Cody's head rested on a pillow and, encouraged by a slight smile from the nurse, he started to read.

• • •

On the drive out to the forest, Jake rode in the cruiser with Lew while Ray followed in his pickup. After driving for about fifteen minutes, Lew checked in with the dispatch center. She reached Marlaine, the night operator.

"Any news from Bruce Peters?" asked Lew.

"He called in to say there's nothing that can't wait until tomorrow, Chief. He's had the Corbin remains transported to the crime lab for an autopsy. Said he'd be back at the site first thing in the morning. He said it took some doing to find someone who can get a vehicle back in there to salvage the snowmobile. He also said to tell you he's hoping you've got Saturday off." Marlaine chuckled. She knew the deal Lew made with Bruce.

"Anything else?"

"The usual speeding ticket and a rear-ender in the Loon Lake Market parking lot. Officer Donovan is handling that. Oh, and Dani left a note saying the FBI guy got here late this afternoon. She helped him set up his computer."

"What FBI guy?"

"You got me," said Marlaine. "That's all she wrote on this note here."

"Okay, I'll deal with that in the morning," said Lew, perplexed. *FBI guy?* Be nice if someone had told her what that was all about.

"Would it be out of line for me to ask why Dr. Osborne has to be at the hospital tonight?" said Jake when she was off the phone. "I thought you said he is retired."

"I don't think he would mind if I told you," said Lew. "He's in a situation somewhat similar to yours. His seven-year-old grandson is in an isolation unit with spinal meningitis. The doctors aren't sure if he'll make it."

To her surprise, Lew's voice wavered and a sob caught in her throat. She could feel tears starting. "Sorry to get emotional. Anyway, Doc's relieving his daughter and her husband so they can grab a bite to eat and check on their daughters—they have two. And, ah, I'm worried for Doc."

"I can tell," said Jake, "and rightly so. Don't apologize."

Lew gave him a thankful grin. "Yeah, it's tough."

• • •

When they reached an entrance to the national forest, Ray's truck pulled ahead. With the map open on the seat beside him, he led the way along a series of roads snaking through the forest. As they drove, the landscape changed from cedar swamps to groves of hardwoods and stretches of evergreens. At no time did they see any other cars, much less the Jeep Wrangler that Liam had been assigned.

"Ray, you got any bars for service on your phone?" asked Lew. "Mine is good."

"Nothing on mine," said Jake.

"That's okay," said Lew. "You'll be with me anyway."

"Two—enough to reach you if I see anything. For sure, I can text," said Ray. "Got your compass? I'm going to walk at a diagonal from you so we're not leaving too large a gap from the territory you're searching."

"That works," said Lew. "Okay, let's see what we can do before it's too late."

She trudged off through a dense stand of balsam with Jake at her heels. They were out of sight within minutes, though Ray could hear them moving through the brush. He checked his compass before taking the diagonal track. He moved slowly hoping to see a sign of a human being having passed through the forest near him. Soon he was in a cathedral of old-growth hemlock where the only sounds were woodland creatures moving in the dim light, tracking him. He smiled. He loved these hidden caves of serenity where the only green beneath the towering spires were the ferns waving seductively across the forest floor. How did it happen that the rapacious loggers of the 1800s had missed these few acres of grand hemlocks? He had a hunch: There must have been a man like himself who saw the glory and the grandeur of the forest—and lied on his maps. Lied to save the trees and their haunted havens.

Lied to save the owls, the woodpeckers—the predators and their prey safe in their universe.

He paused. A familiar fragrance in the air. *Really? Someone smoking weed back in here?* But as suddenly as the smell had hit his nose it was gone with a breeze that blew past him. He waited but the air was crystalline—no hint of marijuana. Finally he shrugged and moved forward. Must have been a flashback to his teenage years when he would sneak into a glen of hemlock not far from his parents' cottage to light up, lay back, and love life. Yeah, it had to have been a flashback.

He spent the next two hours crisscrossing a vast swamp, following deer trails when he could, and hoping he wouldn't stumble into a deep hole of the muck that liked to pretend it was quicksand. Just to be sure, he carried a long, sturdy branch he could use to break a fall or provide some leverage if he was lucky enough to fall close to firm ground. Should that happen, he could signal with a text message, screaming for help. As an added precaution, he pinned his compass up on his shoulder. Moving slowly, he scanned the landscape of swamp grasses, brush, purple loosestrife, and tag alder, hoping every moment that he might spot an unfamiliar shape or evidence that Liam Barber had passed this way. When his flashlight dimmed in need of new batteries and the cloud cover over the moon made it difficult to see, he decided with reluctance to give up for the night.

But it's warm, he thought. *If the kid can find cover, he'll be okay. I'll find him in the morning—and treat him to a Ray Pradt Special of sautéed bluegill and fresh brown eggs. If I really like the kid, he can have a slice of that lemon meringue pie I made yesterday. Yes, that's the ticket. Sleep well tonight, kid, and all will be well in the morning . . . I hope.* Ray refused to let himself think otherwise. He believed in happy endings.

It was ten o'clock when Ray pulled his pickup over to the side of the road, walked back to the cruiser, leaned in through Lew's open window, and said, "Too dark, folks. I think we'll all do better if we get a few hours sleep and start again first thing in the morning. And I have an idea."

He held out the open *Gazetteer* and pointed to a spidery web of county roads, forest roads, logging lanes, and old railroad grades weaving through the national forest. "See this? And this doesn't even show all the new logging lanes or roads recently opened for forest management—we're looking for a needle in a haystack. If you can afford it, Jake, I suggest you let me contact a buddy of mine who owns a small Cessna Skyhawk he charters out of the airport in Rhinelander. Holds four and we can cover a lot more ground—"

"Done. How soon can we start in the morning?"

"Let me call Terry now. If he's not booked, we'll meet him at five A.M. and be in the air as the sun comes up."

• • •

It was after nine when Osborne got home from the hospital. Finding it hard to concentrate, he puttered around making sure the dog had fresh water. He checked his phone at least six times to see if Lew had called. She had not.

He knew the smart thing was to get in bed, maybe read a little—in spite of a nagging sense that he had left something unfinished. Walking into the mudroom to let the dog out for the last time, he spotted the flask of whiskey that he kept on the shelf over the freezer: a reminder he would always be tempted.

To date he was three and a half years recovering. Mary Lee's death had been the trigger that sent him into a lonely, lost haze of alcohol. Even as he treasured the life he had now, he would never forget those days. If his daughters hadn't cared enough to perform the intervention that changed his life, he would have missed getting to know his grandson these past few years.

Thinking about Cody reminded him of how the boy loved to fish. After letting the dog in, Osborne walked through the living room toward his bedroom when a breeze from the porch and a glimpse of a crescent moon changed his mind, luring him down to the water.

He strolled onto the dock, hands thrust deep in his pockets, and stood gazing at a lavender lake quiet but for a lone duck quacking into the stillness. Sinking onto a nearby bench, he thought about the hours he had sat right there showing Cody his fishing tackle and helping him learn to cast the spinning rod he'd bought the boy for his fourth birthday.

When the two of them went out in the boat, Osborne always packed Cody's favorite lunch—never had he seen a kid eat an egg salad sandwich with such gusto. The excitement of catching his first smallmouth bass had Cody jumping up and down and making so much noise that Osborne had to warn him he was scaring all the fish away.

More memories of their times together kept Osborne smiling into the dark. Cody was the boy he had hoped to have years ago. If these times together were all that he was to have—these memories—then that would have to be. Gratitude swelled in his heart. He could deal with the loss another time.

After a while, he looked down at his watch. He had been on the dock for two hours. Osborne got to his feet and started up to the house. Once again the lake had conquered whiskey.

Chapter Fifteen

Lew woke undecided about what to tackle first. On the one hand, she wanted to help with the search for Jake's son; on the other, she had reports from Officers Donovan and Adamczak to review—not to mention calls to the DA if arrests had been made or subpoenas were needed. Staffing for the coming weekend was still to be determined, too.

It was early in the morning and she was thrilled to see her new coffeemaker, a birthday gift from Doc, was dependable as opposed to the old one that had had a mind of its own. The old one drove her nuts. She would set it for six in the morning but it preferred to brew at six in the evening—no matter how carefully she programmed it. But this new one had a feature unique to most coffeemakers: *no programming.* So at 4:45 she pulled on her robe and slippers and padded into the kitchen where she loaded fresh-ground coffee into the basket and proceeded to execute a complex move: She pressed the "on" button. Brushing her teeth, she inhaled the heavenly aroma of fresh-brewed coffee. Ah, the day was off to a fine start.

A full mug of hot coffee in one hand, a manila envelope holding three days of reports from her officers in the other, she walked down to a wide wooden swing at the shoreline. She loved this hour on a mid-summer morning. Birds trilling in the white birches circling her tiny lake (some party poopers called Silver Birch a "pond" but not Lew—she insisted it was a lake), a splash from a smallmouth bass feeding under the lily pads, and a light breeze bearing the fragrance of wildflowers.

Taking a careful sip from the hot mug, she laid the file on the seat beside her and picked up Officer Roger Adamczak's reports. He'd had a call from Joan Frank on Coolidge Lane who was sure she had seen "a strangely dressed man running from the scene of a crime." Roger checked it out—a runner training for the Minocqua Marathon.

Mrs. Kirsch had stopped Roger on Lincoln Street to complain "for the seventh time" that her neighbor's son, Jared, "is parking his beat-up disgusting rusty old pickup, covered with mud splatters, right in front of my lovely home!" She was livid and accused Roger and the Loon Lake Police of taking bribes from Jared's father who managed the local McDonald's. After assuring Mrs. Kirsch that was not the case, Roger went next door where he tried to persuade the kid to park his truck in front of his parents' house but the young man was so high on something Roger wasn't sure he heard.

Lew made a note to Roger that next time Mrs. Kirsch complains he should search the pickup for drugs.

Next she checked the reports from Officer Todd Donovan. He was on night duty that week and twice he arrested two young women who were sleeping in a car parked in front of the TipTop Bar after closing hours. They weren't drunk, they were high and admitted to smoking marijuana they had bought from some boys in the bar earlier. They called it "blueberry" and said they had been high for hours on it. Todd noted that he had confiscated what dope they still had and was sending it in for testing. He made a note that it might be more potent than the marijuana the department had confiscated early in the spring.

Lew refilled her coffee mug and walked back to the swing, thinking. The report from Todd bothered her. This was not the first time she had heard the word "blueberry" and not in connection with someone picking the local fruit. Nearly fifty people—she would have to check the numbers to be exact—had been arrested for possession of marijuana since late April, and they all admitted to buying it from someone who called it "blueberry." Their descriptions of the dealers from whom they made the purchase varied. Some bought from friends (whom they would not identify and Lew didn't blame them), some from women they didn't know, some from men they'd never seen before, and a few said they thought their dealers might have been Hispanic. The good news was the people arrested were for "possession only"—they weren't dealing. The bad news was that someone was. Todd had written in his report that, looking back at all the arrests they had made since spring that, "I think we're looking at an epidemic. I've never seen so much weed so readily available in years."

Lew set his report down. Todd was right. The seventies in Loon Lake had mirrored a national increase in drug use with marijuana and LSD the drugs of choice. But in the eighties and nineties, drug arrests in Loon Lake and the county had been few and far between. The police heard of cocaine and heroin in the cities but rarely in the Northwoods. That had changed in the last five years as meth labs flourished in the region, especially down around Wausau and Stevens Point—but even that had faded recently. Not that it didn't exist but it wasn't driving the Loon Lake's police agenda the way it had previously.

But now this increasing traffic in marijuana—and evidently a high grade of marijuana—was alarming. Maybe it was time to call in the DEA for help. Lew decided to run that by the police chiefs in nearby towns and see if they were having the same problem. Aside from that, she was relieved to find that the officers' reports held nothing that couldn't be handled over the next few days.

Okay. One more cup of coffee after her shower and it would be time to drive into town.

Chapter Sixteen

It was just past six A.M. when Lew pulled the cruiser into her parking space. With a quick wave toward the dispatchers, she walked to her office. To her surprise, the door was locked. It had been a year since the cleaning crew had made that mistake. She fished for her keys and opened it.

Someone had taken over her desk. A laptop computer stood open there, its screen dark. Her desktop computer was missing along with the metal file holder with the manila files containing paperwork for active cases. Even the height of her office chair had been changed to accommodate someone else's legs. Scanning the room to see what else had been disturbed, she spotted an unfamiliar dark green fleece jacket on the coat rack in the corner.

Picking up the phone on her desk, she called the dispatch center. "What's going on? Who's been in my office?"

Before she could say more a slim, dark-haired man about her height walked through the door.

"Me," he said. "I need this space. We moved you across the hall to that big conference room," said the man. "Alan Strickland, FBI." He held out a hand to shake hers.

Ignoring the hand, Lew picked up the laptop from her desk, unplugged it, and shoved it into his arms. "The big conference room? It's all yours. You just let my assistant, Dani, know what else you may need." Before he could answer, Lew bent down to readjust her chair.

"You don't understand. I have a federal case breaking—money laundering."

"I hear what you're saying, Alan, but I have cases breaking, too. Homicide, search and rescue. I need you out of here now."

"I don't think you understand," Strickland said. "This is a *federal* case—and federal trumps local in case you've forgotten."

"I know that," said Lew, "but I have a lot going on right now and your taking over my office is . . . well, it just won't work. Tell you what, Mr. Strickland. How about I set you up in the conference room but also give you full access to my assistant, Dani? She's an expert with computer searches and I'll tell her to help you with anything you may need. Will that work?"

Strickland gave her a long look before acquiescing. "Okay—but if it doesn't work for me, you can count on a call from the regional office with pushback on this." He grabbed his jacket from the coat rack.

"I understand and I'll explain to them everything we have going on here besides your investigation—and I'll suggest they give me a heads up next time. I don't think that is too much to ask, do you?"

Strickland exhaled in frustration. "All right. But may I bother you with one question? Do you have time for that?"

"Shoot," said Lew.

She walked past him to rescue her computer from the conference room. Her computer was still on a wheeled cart with the file holder on the shelf below. With Strickland following her, she wheeled the cart out of the conference room and back where it belonged. Strickland tagged along behind.

"I'm looking for a Herbert L. Jarvison," he said. "Ever heard of the guy? I can't find him in the Loon Lake phone book and a search online gives me only a B. and N. Jarvison. I'm about to try the DMV—"

"Oh, sure. You mean Bud Jarvison. That online number should be correct. Is that it?" She made the question sound like a door slamming shut.

"Yes, thank you."

When the door had closed behind him, Lew clicked on her computer. Waiting for it to boot up, she mulled over the confrontation with Strickland. She cautioned herself to reserve judgment but right now she didn't like the guy. Didn't like his looks with the flat, pursed lips and dark eyes too close together. And she didn't like his taking over her office without asking. Would he have done that to a man in her position? What a weasel.

She glanced up at the wall clock. Doc had a habit of dropping in for one last cup of coffee after meeting with his McDonald's buddies. She was hoping to hear there had been some improvement in Cody's condition.

The phone rang and the dispatcher said a woman was on the line with an emergency call for Lew. She was refusing to give any details other than her name and that she was a nurse with the Office of Public Health with information on Liam's missing car.

"I'll take it," said Lew. "Hello, this is Chief Ferris."

"Kathy Winter here," said a female voice, shaking as she spoke. "I am sorry to call so early but I had stopped in at the sheriff's department late yesterday afternoon and saw the alert for that missing Jeep. Our offices are down the hall and I was giving one of the secretaries a ride home. It didn't register at first, but I woke up in the middle of the night and realized I may have seen that car. Twice in the last two days. I drove by the office early this morning to write down the license number and then I just now drove out there to check the car and I'm sure—"

"Where?" Lew got to her feet. "This is an emergency, Kathy. Where did you see the car?"

"You have to promise me one thing or I can't tell you."

"What? We have a missing person whose life is at risk."

"I know, I know. But I've been meeting this migrant family to treat their little boy for an infected deer tick bite. We meet near a crossroads on Spider Lake Road and Forest Road 2716. Out in the Nicolet National Forest."

"You better tell me right now where this car is," said Lew, "or you will be cited for interfering with an investigation."

"The child's parents are undocumented—illegal immigrants. They are terrified they'll be caught and arrested. I had to promise them I wouldn't turn them in or they wouldn't let me treat the little boy."

"I am not interested in the family," said Lew. "Is that what you need to hear?"

Lew heard a sigh of relief on the line and the woman said, "I'm parked at the Pine Tree Diner. I'll wait for you here and take you to the car 'cause you won't find it otherwise. It's parked off a forest road—"

"I'm on my way," said Lew. She dashed for the door, nearly knocking Osborne over as he walked in.

Chapter Seventeen

"How's the little guy doing, Doc?" asked Lew as they walked together toward the entrance to the police department.

"No change as of this morning," said Osborne. "But new tests are being run today. A resident thinks he's found evidence of a strep in the bloodstream so that is being checked out. If that's the case, they will start antibiotics. Erin and Mark are counting on me to relieve them at four. I'm hoping we'll have better news by then."

"Good. And I appreciate your driving along with me this morning."

"Happy to do it."

Osborne stopped at his car to grab the black medical bag in which he carried forms needed to draft a death certificate, as well as extra pairs of Nitrile gloves and a random assortment of dental instruments. Neither he nor Lew cared to state the worst out loud but they both knew that five days with no word from Liam Barber was not promising.

"Excuse me for a minute, Doc," said Lew as she pulled onto the shoulder. "I've been trying to reach Ray and Jake. I tried Ray a few minutes ago, left a message, but he hasn't called back. They're up doing an aerial search. I hope they don't have to fly all the way back to Rhinelander before they meet up with us."

This time she reached Jake on his cell phone. The pilot of the small Cessna responded that he could bring his plane down on a private landing strip at the casino not far from the diner.

"Good," said Lew. "You'll be less than ten miles away. Meet us at the Pine Tree Diner—Ray knows where it's at."

"I'm glad that public health nurse is meeting us out here," said Osborne. "I've hunted partridge in those woods and I have always been grateful for my compass. Even the annual update of the *Gazetteer* is obsolete when it comes to finding your way around the national forest. What they call 'forest roads' in that damn guide all look like deer trails to me."

Twenty-five minutes later, Lew and Doc pulled into a gravel parking area in front of the diner. Four cars were parked there already, including a small red Toyota SUV. As Lew opened her car door, a woman jumped out of the Toyota and ran over to her.

"I'm Kathy Winter," she said. "Ready?"

"Give us a few minutes," said Lew. "We have two more people on their way. Should be here any minute."

As she was speaking, Jake's Navigator skidded into the parking area. He and Ray hurried over to where Lew and Osborne stood with the anxious-looking nurse Winter. Osborne was relieved to see Jake had traded the business suit for worn jeans and a blue shirt with the sleeves rolled up—much better for a rigorous search over challenging terrain.

"Are you the one who found my son's car?" asked Jake after a quick round of introductions.

"I'm pretty sure it's the one the sheriff's been looking for. I drove out here an hour ago to check the license plate. Yes, I'm sure."

"How far from here?" asked Jake.

"Less than a mile but off this county road a bit so follow me," said Kathy.

After turning off the paved county road, the three cars bounced and lurched down a bumpy two-lane road until the red Toyota slowed to a stop. Kathy got out and pointed to the spot just ahead of her vehicle. Tucked back in a clearing and a good twenty feet from the road was a rusty Jeep Wrangler.

Jake ran to the car and yanked the driver's side door open. He leaned in, fumbling around in the interior as Lew and Osborne walked up behind him. Ray, meanwhile, ambled up and down the road, feet slow but eyes on the grasses banding a wall of young aspen. As he neared the old Jeep, Lew walked over to him and said in a whisper, "Don't forget your camera."

"The keys are in the ignition," said Jake, backing out of the car. "I found Liam's wallet. He likes to hide it under the front seat." He waved the wallet in the air before handing it to Lew. He turned to the nurse who was leaning against her car. "I can't thank you enough—what did you say your name is?"

"Kathy Winter. I feel so bad. I saw this car three days ago but I didn't think—"

"Hey, you guys," said Ray. "Get over here." He pointed past the grasses. "We've got footprints in the sand heading in that direction. Might be tough going through this aspen. Jake, roll down those sleeves and watch you don't get poked in the eye. Ready?"

"If you don't need me anymore, I have to be on my way to check on my patients," said Kathy.

"The migrant family?" asked Lew.

Kathy nodded as she climbed back into her car. "Yes, so far no Lyme disease."

Half a mile into the woods, which had given way to a cedar swamp, Ray raised a hand for them to stop. "Hear that?" It was the sound of water. "We can't be far."

They trudged on, Lew behind Ray, Jake behind her, and Osborne bringing up the rear. Fifteen minutes passed before Ray paused again. He beckoned to Lew and leaned over to whisper. She nodded and fell back.

"Jake, Ray thinks you should wait here while he checks—"

Too late. Jake had spotted the white T-shirt with the green emblem of the Natural Resources Society. "Oh, God," he said, leaping across the swampy hummocks of grass and tag alder bordering the river. He stopped short of the still form.

Liam's body rested face down in the branches of a tag alder bush. His arms were splayed out and his knees sagged beneath him. Four days in the July son had taken a toll on the body. Death hung in the air, a miserable fragrance. Flies buzzed.

"Don't go any farther," said Lew, her voice cautious. "Please. You may disturb the site."

"I won't. Don't worry. But stay back for a few minutes, will you?"

No one moved. A grasshopper shrilled. The river burbled. Tears coursed down the father's face. Finally he said, "Is that . . . is that a bullet wound on the side of his head?"

"I'm standing too far away to say for sure," said Osborne though he was darn sure he was looking at damage that could only be done by a rifle. "I'll take a closer look when Chief Ferris gives the okay."

"Jake," said Lew, "please, I can only imagine how you must be feeling right now but we'll have to have the crime lab experts examine your son's body in order to know exactly what has happened here."

Jake nodded and stumbled back.

Lew beckoned to Ray. "Photos please."

"Doc," said Lew after Ray had waded into the shallows to take photos from all angles, "no question the victim took a bullet in the head. Would you agree with me the entrance wound is behind the left ear?"

"Yes," said Osborne, "but you'll want Bruce to confirm. I'm recording cause of death as homicide."

"Jake," said Lew, "if it helps at all, I'm sure your son died instantly. He never . . ."

As she spoke, she and Doc turned to look at Jake. He was crouched over his knees, arms folded tight over his head. A look passed between Lew and Osborne: They both knew despair. After a long while, Jake raised his head and stood up. He wiped at his face and stepped forward.

"May I now?" he asked Lew.

She nodded.

As Jake bent to lay a comforting arm over his son's body, Osborne tugged at Lew's sleeve. Eight feet away on the sandy river bank and nearly hidden from view by grasses was a fly rod Osborne guessed to be about fourteen feet long. Tied at one end was a bright pink fluorocarbon fishing line, which bobbed in the water along the shoreline.

Pulling on a pair of Nitrile gloves, Lew reached for the rod. At the end of the pink line was tied three feet of tippet and at the end of that was one of the few trout flies Osborne could recognize: a Royal Wulff. Rod in one hand, Lew moved along the riverbank, bending to search through the grasses.

"The reel should be here somewhere . . ."

"No reel used on a tenkara rod," said Jake. "Chief Ferris, is it okay for me to check the pockets on Liam's vest? He kept his trout flies in a little wooden box. I'd hate for that to be lost."

"Go right ahead," said Lew. "I'm about to call Bruce Peters who is the Wausau Crime Lab's top investigator. I'll arrange for Bruce to take your son's body down to the crime lab for an autopsy. Required when death is from unnatural causes."

"I understand," said Jake. "I have been preparing myself for this. I guess—I would hope his body could be returned to me in Illinois. Actually, no. I would like him returned to Loon Lake and maybe you folks can recommend a funeral home. I want him cremated. That way I can take his ashes to one of the rivers we fished in Wyoming. Liam would like that."

"Bruce?" Lew had walked away from the riverbank, hoping she might get a cell signal. Otherwise she wouldn't be able to make the call until after hiking the mile back to the squad car. But Bruce answered.

"Yeah, Chief Ferris, no news on those remains yet—"

"That's not why I'm calling. I have a new victim and crime scene—you're going to have a long day I'm afraid."

After giving him the details, Lew said, "I'm staying here with the victim's father. Doc will hike back to my squad car, meet you at the Pine Tree Diner, and bring you here. I'm pretty sure it's a head wound from a rifle and the body has not been in water so that may help. Ray Pradt is here, too. I'm asking him to check the perimeters for any tracks or signs of the shooter. He's taken photos, too."

"Okay, Chief. One thing on that snowmobiler I think you would appreciate knowing. Remember how the skull is caved in on one side?"

"Yes."

"I checked it against the damaged helmet—the patterns match. That victim was wearing the helmet when he suffered the trauma that fractured his skull. He was shot."

"Rifle or shotgun?"

"That I don't know. Likely impossible to tell but interesting, huh?"

Chapter Eighteen

Osborne got to the hospital early and headed straight for the reception desk to check in, a requirement because Cody was in isolation and only immediate family members were allowed to visit. To his chagrin, Bud was sitting in the waiting room. Up on his feet faster than Osborne had seen him move in years, he called Osborne over.

"Say, Doc, how's your grandson?"

"Not sure yet, Bud, I just got here. Excuse me—I need to check with the receptionist."

"No, wait. Did you hear about Pete Corbin?" Before Osborne could answer, Bud said, "You know he worked in one of our banks. Nice, nice fella."

"Vaguely remember the family, Bud. Excuse me, my daughter and son-in-law are waiting."

"Word on the street is poor Pete had a few too many, took that sled out, and boom! Right through the ice. That's what Chief Ferris must think, right?" Bud's right knee kept up a steady jiggle as he spoke.

"Bud, I don't have time for this right now. Now if you will please excuse me."

"Sure, sure. I called over to the police department today for information. You know, corporate wants to do something for the family now that we know what happened to the poor guy."

Osborne turned to the receptionist, hoping to escape to Cody's room as soon as possible.

"Yeah, the woman from the dispatcher center over at the police station told me you and Chief Ferris were out in the Nicolet National Forest all day." Bud raised his eyebrows, a nasty glint in his eye. "So, Doc, what the heck is going on? You two taking a little time off? Fishing of course?" He winked. "I wouldn't blame you. She's a nice-looking gal."

Osborne wasn't sure what angered him more, the idiot's nosiness or his unwholesome interest in the nature of Osborne's relationship with Lewellyn Ferris.

"No funny business if that's what you mean," said Osborne, his voice curt. "A missing person report and I was deputized should there be a need for a coroner's report since Pecore is having surgery this week. If you want to know more, I'm sure you can hear all about it on Channel 12 tonight."

The receptionist handed Osborne a room pass to show the nurse. Before he could leave the waiting room, Bud blocked his way. "Really, a missing person? Where?"

"Damn it, Bud, get out of my way. Told you I do not have time for this. Now move."

The look of hurt and surprise on Bud's face caught Osborne off guard.

"I am sorry," said Bud, backing away. He threw his hands up in surrender. "I'm just an old man stuck here waiting to hear how my poor wife is doing. I have no business asking you all these questions. I am so very sorry, Paul. Please, I apologize."

The expression of apology seemed so sincere that Osborne felt guilty for his own rudeness. He relented. After all, wouldn't it be just as easy to answer Bud's questions and leave it at that? Take him a minute at most. Then he could be on his way and no one's feelings would be hurt.

"One of the public health nurses helped us locate a student who went missing while researching invasive plant species."

"You're kidding. A public health nurse out in the national forest? Where in the forest?" Bud's voice tightened. "What the hell would she be doing out there?"

Now *that* was none of Bud's business. Kathy Winter had been determined to protect the migrant family whose child she was treating. Osborne gave him a curious look. This questioning was a bit much even for a lonely man waiting to see his ailing wife.

He was about to ask why Bud would care *where* in the forest when a familiar voice said, "Yo, Doc. Am I too late for visiting hours? Got a surprise for someone you know." Ray loped into the visiting room.

Osborne did a double take. Cocked at a crazy angle on Ray's head was a miniature version of his hat with the stuffed trout.

"Ray, how did you get back so soon?" asked Osborne.

"One of the techs from the crime lab had to come back to town for supplies. I hitched a ride. Lew said to let you know she'll call when they head back. And this"—he removed the fish from his head—"is a gift for your grandson."

He handed Osborne the hat, which was an exact copy of his, down to a shiny new fishing lure draped with care across the body of the trout. "Kaye made it up for me," he said, referring to the elderly friend he kept supplied with fresh bluegills in return for the care and feeding of his precious hats (summer and winter versions).

"Say, you jack pine savage," Bud interrupted. "You still living in that crummy house trailer out on Loon Lake?"

"Oh, golly, if it isn't the talking boulder," said Ray, his voice cheery as he batted back the remark. "Speaking of lifestyles, how's that place of yours? The yard with the toy trees."

A confused look crossed Bud's face. Osborne realized he was unaware that some residents of Loon Lake considered Nancy's aggressively landscaped lawn to be as fake as her smile.

"Come on, you two," said Osborne with an attempt at a chuckle. "You know you love each other."

Bud shrugged. "So, Pradt, what do you suggest for crappies on a hot day like today? Might take my boat out later." Getting to his feet, Bud hitched up the golf shorts he was wearing.

"The Lil' Hustler spinner baits have been working for me," said Ray. "I change colors 'til I find ones they like. By the way, if you're looking to invest some of those millions you got, I'm working on developing an app for muskie fishing. Got this teenager buddy of mine who's a whiz of a developer. We're putting in the best locations, size of fish caught and when, the baits used, even the time of day. Could be mega bucks."

"Now why would I throw money at a guy with a fish on his head?" asked Bud as he walked toward the exit. He paused and turned to look hard at Ray. Shaking a finger at him, Bud said, "You know what I think every time I see you in that stupid hat? If my son had lived, he would have made something of his life."

Before Ray could open his mouth Bud had disappeared.

"Whoa, what was that all about?" said Ray after Bud was gone.

"Not sure," said Osborne. "But Nancy Jarvison is here recovering from shoulder surgery so I think he's out of sorts a bit. I'm glad you walked in when you did. He was bugging me for information about Lew."

"Planning to hit on her, maybe. Wouldn't surprise me—he's getting a little long in the tooth for the young ones."

"I wouldn't go that far," said Osborne. "Old Bud may be a practiced adulterer but he knows his type and I doubt Lew is it. No, he was less interested in Lew than in what she was *doing*, what the two of us were—"

"Dr. Osborne, sorry to interrupt," said the woman sitting at the reception desk in the far corner. "I couldn't help overhearing you and I thought you might like to know that Mrs. Jarvison went home yesterday."

"She did? Then why was he here?"

"I assumed he was waiting for you," said the woman. "Wasn't he?"

Chapter Nineteen

Lew sat on a fallen log, finishing up her notes while Bruce and a colleague worked their way around the body, scouring the shoreline and river shallows for evidence. "Chief, did Ray find anything when he walked the perimeter?"

Lew glanced up. "No, no signs whatsoever. At least not yet. He thinks it was a rifle shot from quite a distance. I've asked him to take time tomorrow to walk farther out, a good half-mile if he can."

She turned to Jake, who was sitting on a stump a short distance away watching as his son's body was slipped into a body bag for transport to the crime lab in Wausau. "Jake, you and Ray didn't happen to see anything unusual when you were up in the plane today, did you? Any indication of people living back in here? Tents? Shacks? I know where the campgrounds are and none are close to this area."

"We were up on the far end where Liam had been working his square on the grid. I'd say a good five miles or so from there—so, no, we didn't fly over this area."

Bruce walked over to where they were sitting and knelt beside Jake. "Mr. Barber, your son never knew what hit him. I am confident the bullet entered from behind. He died instantly with the force of the bullet throwing his body forward."

"Thank you," said Jake. "Based on what I've seen here, I'll bet you anything my son was in the midst of a cast with his tenkara rod. That means he died with his heart full of anticipation. And look around us," said Jake with a wave of his arm. "Think of where he was at that moment: standing in a pool of sunlight, watching the ripples on the river, hearing the whispers of these magnificent pines. If death has to happen," his voice cracked, "could there be a better place to die?"

Lew turned to him with a soft smile. "I wish I could have felt that when I lost my son."

"You lost a child?" asked Jake.

Bruce sat on the grass near Lew, legs akimbo as he listened.

"He was seventeen and a troubled kid." She resisted adding *too much like his father*. Instead she said, "Knifed in a bar fight. On a dark night in a parking lot."

Jake thought that over before asking, "How did you feel at the time?"

"Numb . . . and a failure as a parent."

"Hmm," said Jake.

"But my grandfather to whom I was very close—the person who taught me how to fly-fish—knew how to help me in my grief. He made me go fishing."

"He did?" asked Jake, taken aback.

"Yep. I waded into the trout stream near my grandfather's place where I had fished as a kid and I stayed in that water for two whole weeks. Gramps said the water would heal me. And it did. At least I came out a whole person."

"I know you mentioned earlier that you fly-fish," said Jake.

"She doesn't just fly-fish—she's the expert," said Bruce. "She taught me everything I know from casting to fly tying. That's why I finagle to get assigned up here. Get a lesson every time." He smirked in satisfaction. "Getting one this weekend, right?"

"You nut," said Lew, batting at his head. "Yes, of course."

"I have an idea," said Jake. "I have to stay in Loon Lake until my son's body is released from the crime lab, right? And I am thinking I may have him cremated while I'm up here, too. So, have you two ever tried tenkara fishing?"

"Never heard of it until we met you," said Lew. "Have you, Bruce?"

"Nope."

"I'll teach you. We'll use Liam's rod and I'll have my office courier up my equipment. If the weather holds, we'll give it a try Friday. Right here on the Pine where my son . . ."

"I would like that very much," said Lew.

"What about me? Can I tag along?" asked Bruce, looking more like a twelve-year-old kid than a forensic scientist nearing age thirty.

"That reminds me," said Jake. "I searched all through Liam's fishing vest and I could not find the wooden box he carried his trout flies in. He only ever had two flies in the box. It's only this big and not heavy." Jake held out two fingers.

"That's too bad. He may have been holding it and it flew out of his hand when he was hit," said Bruce. He looked toward where his colleague was finishing up near the tag alder where Liam died. "I'll take a close look all around over there before we head back today."

"Thank you," said Jake.

As they walked back through the forest to their vehicles, Jake said, "Chief Ferris, I would like to find the Catholic Church in Loon Lake. Can you tell me where it is?"

"Doc attends Mass several times a week. I'll have him give you a call. I'm not sure what the daily schedule is."

Chapter Twenty

Returning to the station, Lew was relieved to find her office empty and her desk just as she had left it. She poked her head into the conference room where the weasel sat hunched over his laptop. "Alan," she said, "any luck? How's it going?"

He looked up and pushed his chair back. "Actually, yes. I reached a local bank officer who was able to tell me all about your friend."

"My friend?" Lew walked into the room, crossed her arms, and waited.

"Mr. Jarvison. Bud."

"I know the man. He is not my friend."

"Oh well," Alan smirked, "whatever. Turns out Chairman Jarvison has been making deposits to his personal bank account every few days in amounts just below the legal limit of ten grand that triggers SARs—Suspicious Activity Reports."

"How much money are you talking about?"

"At the rate he's been depositing? Forty to fifty thousand a week. And staying just under the radar we use to target money launderers."

"So *that's* why you're here," said Lew. "I've been wondering what would bring the FBI to Loon Lake. The Jarvisons are very wealthy people. He inherited millions and since he's retired from the day-to-day operations maybe it's an oversight. Probably thought he didn't have to worry about it."

"Doubt that. Fact is our regional office was tipped off about this activity months ago. Last December, in fact. But we had to prioritize Homeland Security directives so I didn't get around to checking on this until I saw the posting about the banker found dead in your national forest."

"You mean Peter Corbin?"

"I remembered the name the minute I saw it. He's the banker who tipped us. He said that he brought the issue of the multiple deposits to Mr. Jarvison's attention because he didn't want the Jarvison Bank Corporation held accountable and fined. All he asked at the time was that Jarvison document the source of his funds in order to keep the transactions transparent for bank regulators. Up until then, he assumed Jarvison was selling stocks. When Jarvison blew him off, he had second thoughts and came to us."

"You think Bud Jarvison had something to do with Peter Corbin's death?"

Alan's eyes searched Lew's. "I wouldn't go that far—yet. The first question is where is the money coming from?"

"That's easy to answer. The family is filthy rich."

"*Was* filthy rich."

Lew pulled out a chair and sat down. "Now how do you know that?" The guy might look like a weasel but she was impressed with his work ethic. "Is the bank allowed to share personal financial information?"

"I didn't need it. I used the old 'hunting and fishing' technique: talked to a stockbroker who duck hunts with the banker and was an advisor to Jarvison until very recently. He said Jarvison made some really big and really bad bets in the market last year. Lost $32 million."

Lew whistled. "So what next?"

"Like I said—I need to find the source of that money. Is he laundering from someone or some group? Is it mob money?

Wouldn't be the first time that's happened up here. Yep, I'm looking for the source."

Lew said, "We found another victim in the Nicolet National Forest today. That makes two bodies in an area so remote that few people hunt, fish, or camp in there. Plus it's a wolf rendezvous site so it's dangerous to be in there alone."

Alan studied her. "Sorry I disturbed your office. I had no idea you have so much happening in this town."

Lew waved a hand. "Don't worry about it. Does Jarvison know you're looking into this?"

"Not yet. Please don't say anything to anyone. I need to learn the source of the cash before I confront him—or his wife. Both their names are on the deposit slips."

• • •

Not until Osborne was driving home late that night did it occur to him the one question Bud did not ask: *What happened to the missing student?*

Chapter Twenty-One

The owl swiveled his majestic snowy-white head to stare at Osborne, amber eyes boring into the doc's. Was the owl trying to tell him something? Before Osborne could ask, the bird flew a few feet away. He landed in fog with his back to Osborne. The air felt chilled. Osborne started to follow him but the bird kept hopping just ahead. Osborne noticed that the owl's wings had disappeared and the big white head had the body of a small boy and the boy kept just ahead of Osborne, walking with the firm footsteps of a fearless child.

Osborne could see a hand pulling the boy-owl. A hand that belonged to a snowman—a snowman who towered over the boy. The two beings stopped and looked back at Osborne. The owl's eyes blazed and seemed to pulse with meaning. Osborne was sure he should be seeing or hearing some message. He reached out both hands, begging for more information, but the boy-owl turned his back again. Again the snowman pulled the boy-owl along.

Only now the snowman was growing larger, the boy-owl smaller. Osborne wanted to call out for them to wait for him but his voice wouldn't work. Even at a distance Osborne could see the snowman was missing the back half of his head. It didn't seem to bother the snowman. He wasn't bleeding. *But of course not,* thought Osborne, *snowmen don't bleed.*

Just as he questioned why an owl would have a boy's body and why an owl would walk not fly, the air changed. Grew warm, then hot. The owl shed its body and charged Osborne, the eyes a lurid greenish-yellow as it hovered in front of his face. Osborne struggled to know what the eyes were trying to tell him.

As fast as it had come at him, the owl flew off. It landed and again the pristine white head floated on the body of a boy. And again the boy-owl held tight to the hand of a tall figure as the two walked away. This time the figure was not the snowman but someone wearing a white T-shirt emblazoned with a familiar bright green logo: the emblem of the Natural Resources Society.

Osborne chastised himself. He should have known. It's Jake's son, Liam Barber. He's rescuing the boy-owl, keeping him safe. Showing him the way.

• • •

Osborne woke from the dream in a heavy sweat. He pushed the coverlet away and stared up at the ceiling, thinking back on the details of the dream. Why a snowy owl? Then he remembered Cody's favorite hand puppet: a white-feathered snowy owl. But why the snowman with half his head gone? And why that poor young man whom they just found shot to death?

He decided to sit up, drink some water from the glass on the bedside table, and try to make his heart stop pounding. The digital readout on the clock radio indicated it was only three A.M. Mike was sleeping soundly on his dog bed in the corner of the bedroom. Osborne lay back down, his eyes wide open. He knew the significance of the dream and it broke his heart. It would be difficult to wait for sunrise but he would and then he had to see his daughter: Erin had to know.

When he woke three hours later, he was surprised that he had fallen back asleep. Yet even as he slept he knew his heart was telling him something. He hoped he was wrong, but he doubted it.

Chapter Twenty-Two

He arrived at the hospital just as the breakfast trays were being delivered. Erin was on the cot in Cody's room and sitting up with a disposable gown over her robe reading a newspaper when Osborne tapped on the door.

"How's our boy?" whispered Osborne. He had pulled on his gown and mask before entering.

"Still sleeping, Dad. Why are you here so early? No need to whisper. The nurse will be in to wake Cody any minute so he's alert, we hope, when the medical team does its rounds this morning." She adjusted herself on the cot and patted a spot for Osborne to sit.

He walked over, gave her a kiss on the cheek, and sat down. "Where's Mark?"

"He slept at home with the girls. He'll make them some breakfast then come on over."

Osborne took a deep breath, then said, "I think we need to prepare ourselves for the worst, sweetheart." He pressed fingers against his eyelids and hoped he could continue. "I, well, I don't have a good feeling about how Cody can pull through is all."

Erin reached to take his hand. "Dad, of course you don't. You lost your mother just this way. I'm surprised that you hadn't told me this before."

"Really? Erin, you are a stronger person than I am."

"No, Dad, but Mark and I have had each other to hold onto these past days. You didn't have anyone. You were so young when Grandma died." Erin gave his hand a squeeze. "I'm not saying this is easier for us, I'm just saying we know the danger up front. Maybe that helps, maybe we'll find that it doesn't. But, Dad, you are not telling me something I don't already know."

Osborne paused. He had just caught sight of a basket in the corner holding Cody's favorite toys. The hat from Ray sat on top of the white head of the owl hand puppet. The owl's eyes were a light, pleasant yellow this morning.

"All right then," said Osborne, getting to his feet. He bent over to give his daughter a hug. Cody stirred under his blankets. "Is that a good sign?"

"Don't know, Dad. Let's hope."

Seeing Erin lifted his spirits and he walked out of the hospital feeling a little more settled. Maybe it was the benign expression in the puppet owl's eyes. Maybe it was his daughter's strength in the face of the unknown. He reminded himself that every day of his life and the lives of the people around him was an unknown.

Chapter Twenty-Three

Shortly before eight the next morning, Jake and Osborne slipped sideways into Osborne's usual pew and knelt to pray. The church was nearly empty, not unusual for a sunny Saturday morning; most parishioners would attend one of the Sunday Masses.

After Mass had ended, Jake said, "Doc, do you mind waiting for me to talk to the priest? I'd like to arrange to have Liam's ashes blessed before I leave town."

"Not at all," said Osborne, "take your time." While Jake spoke to the priest in the vestibule of the church, Osborne occupied himself reading the parish notices pinned to the church bulletin board.

"All set?" asked Osborne when Jake had shaken hands with the priest. "I'll show you one of Loon Lake's best breakfast spots if you'd like—"

Before he could say more, a female voice called to them from the street in front of the church. Nancy Jarvison was half out of her car and waving madly in their direction. She ran toward them, both hands out.

"Oh, Mr. Barber, I saw you interviewed on the news last evening and I am so sorry to hear what happened to your son." She reached to pump his hand with enthusiasm. "I'm Nancy Jarvison and so pleased to meet you."

"Thank you," said Jake, sounding overwhelmed. "Do you know Dr. Osborne?" he asked turning toward Osborne.

"Of course, his late wife Mary Lee was one of my closest friends. I still miss her, Paul. And how is that little grandson of yours doing?" Before Osborne could open his mouth, she said, "Paul will tell you we lost our only child, our son, in a terrible accident not long ago. Right, Paul?"

Mystified as to what she was up to, Osborne nodded in agreement. He was tempted to mention that the accident was at least fifteen years ago but thought better of it. At the same time, he couldn't help but notice how well put together Nancy was for so early in the morning. She was wearing white pants and a navy blue pullover that highlighted her blond hair and deep summer tan. Even the sling holding her injured shoulder was in a colorful pattern.

Looking up at Jake, she said, "So, Mr. Barber—"

"Jake, just call me Jake."

"Certainly. Jake, you must be wondering how I knew to find you here."

"Well, now that you mention it—"

"The clerk at the inn said you would be attending Mass. The reason I've tracked you down is my husband and I—knowing you must have to stay in town for a few days—we would like you to join us for dinner tonight. Nothing fancy—just ourselves and you . . . and Dr. Osborne."

Osborne could tell he was an afterthought. He also could not think of a place he would like less to be.

"I'm really not up for anything social," said Jake, his voice kind. "But I appreciate the thought."

"Of course you aren't, and we understand." Nancy leaned in and in a low voice said, "I know you run All Tech, Jake. We have been major stockholders for years—only one percent of course. I'm surprised you don't recognize me from the last stockholders meeting."

Jake raised his eyebrows. "Mrs. Jarvison, there were 5,000 people there."

"But we were in the second row."

"Oh? Well . . ."

"So you'll come. Seven this evening. Don't bring a thing except our friend Paul here. And he knows the way." She flashed a bright smile and was back in her car before the two men could close their mouths.

"How the hell did that happen?" asked Jake as the car sped away.

"I learned a long time ago not to get in that woman's way," said Osborne. "Hey, we have the rest of the morning to figure out an excuse not to go."

"Not sure if I shouldn't go. One percent is $10 million. That is a significant investment in our company. Let me think it over." He smiled at Osborne as he said, "I have become intimate with the menu at the Loon Lake Inn. Be nice to have a change. Anyway, she seems a gracious woman."

When she wants to be, thought Osborne, a thought he kept to himself.

After breakfast, Osborne dropped Jake back at the inn and sped to the hospital. Cody's room was sunny and the little guy was propped up on pillows, his eyes open as he listened to his mother reading from a book.

"Dad," Erin jumped to her feet as he walked into the room. "Great news. They found Cody does have a strep in his bloodstream and the antibiotics are working." She brushed strands of hair back from Cody's forehead and leaned down to give him a kiss. "He's drowsy but feeling better. If this continues, he may be able to come home soon."

"Grandpa," said Cody in a small voice. "Will you read me that *Lunker* book again?"

"You bet. Erin, would you like me to take over this afternoon?" asked Osborne.

His daughter nodded happily and they agreed Osborne would take the one to four shift. "I can stay later," he said, hoping for an excuse to avoid the Jarvisons.

"No, but thanks, Dad. We're going to have the girls come up and finally get some family time this evening."

As he drove by the police department on his way home, Osborne was surprised to see Lew's cruiser in the parking lot. That was unusual, as she usually took Saturdays off. He pulled in to tell her about Cody.

The light in Lew's eyes when she caught sight of him made his day even sunnier.

"Whew, isn't that a relief," she said when he had finished sharing the good news about Cody. "Sit down and pour yourself a cup of coffee. I'm just hanging in here hoping to catch up with reports and e-mails that I've let slide the previous two days. Did you take Jake to Mass this morning? How's he doing? I need to let him know that the autopsy is scheduled for Monday. Sorry to make him wait so long."

When she heard about Nancy's invitation, she sat back in her chair, a serious thought clouding her face. "Very interesting. *Very* interesting, Doc. Had a long talk with Alan Strickland, the FBI agent, at the end of the day yesterday. If you have a few minutes, it's time I give you more details on his fraud investigation. You know the Jarvisons and may be able to give him some background that may help.

"Turns out they were tipped months ago by Peter Corbin that he was concerned that the Jarvison Bank Corporation was being compromised by deposits of cash—as much as $40,000 a week— that were being made by Bud Jarvison without documenting the source of the funds. Corbin was concerned that the corporation could be accused of money laundering. Because Corbin, as a bank executive, was responsible for answering to the federal regulators he was trying to protect himself as well as the bank.

"The FBI didn't follow up at the time, Alan said, because they had Homeland Security issues to deal with. It wasn't until he saw the news that Corbin had been found dead that he went back to check on that tip.

"So he's here to investigate Bud Jarvison. He met with Chuck Carlson, president of the local Jarvison bank, yesterday and was told that Bud treats the bank like it's his personal wallet and anyone who questions his decisions gets fired.

"The question Alan has and what he hopes to answer before he confronts Bud is where is the money coming from?" Lew paused and, tipping her head as she asked with a smug smile, "What do you think, Doc?"

"I would assume he's selling some of their millions of dollars' worth of assets and thinks he's above paperwork. The guy is richer than God and used to running the whole show."

"That's exactly what I said to Alan," said Lew. "And that is when he said that he met with Herb Strong, who is Chuck's hunting buddy and was a broker for Jarvison up until last year. Bud lost millions in the stock market. Against Herb's advice, he made bad bets with hedge funds and hi-tech start-ups, crap investments recommended by some old college buddies. Herb estimated Bud's losses had to be in the $30 to $40 million range."

"That could be his entire fortune," said Osborne.

"Makes for an interesting dinner party, don't you think? I'd like you to go, Doc. See if you pick up on anything. Alan would appreciate that, I'm sure. On the other hand, Doc, the Jarvisons are friends of yours. I don't want to put you in a compromising position."

"Oh, I would not say they're friends. My late wife would but I have never wanted to spend time with those people. Jake is likely to go. Nancy made it clear they own a ton of stock in his company but I was hoping to wrangle my way out of the evening."

Lew leaned forward, a wide grin on her face. "What if I asked you to be really rude and invite me along? I would love to go. Frankly, I'm still peeved that Mr. FBI thought he could step in and take over my office. That might change the dynamic around here."

"I'll call ahead and let them know we'll be three."

"I have a better idea. Let's pull a Ray Pradt," she said, referring to Ray's habit of showing up for dinner or a picnic at Osborne's with any number of unexpected guests—generally bearded, scruffy, and pleasant enough but lacking any evidence of good dental hygiene.

"That might catch Nancy off guard," said Osborne, not unhappy at the thought. "Lately Bud has been asking about you so often, I think he'll be tickled to see you."

"Are you serious? I find that strange."

"That he's interested in you? I'm interested in you. Maybe his taste is improving."

Lew blushed.

Osborne reached for his cell phone. "I'm calling Jake to let him know I'll pick him up at 6:45—after I get you. My place tonight?"

"Sure."

Osborne knew he looked the happiest he had all week.

Chapter Twenty-Four

As he guided Lew and Jake into the foyer of the mansion, Osborne glanced through the French doors that opened to the formal dining room. Crystal wineglasses sparkled in the sunlight pouring through floor-to-ceiling windows. White linen napkins were artfully arranged on ornate china plates and silver pitchers held colorful bouquets. This was no outdoor barbecue: Nancy was putting on her best show.

Osborne was glad he had decided to reach into his closet for dress pants he had not worn in months. Now that he didn't have to be in an office every day he lived in jeans and khakis better suited for the boat than a dinner party.

He was doubly pleased when Lew arrived at his place looking elegant in a silky black sleeveless top with matching pants. The outfit emphasized her sturdy, well-toned figure, which reminded Osborne how lucky he was that she had promised to spend the night at his place.

That thought was interrupted by a throaty voice from behind. "Jake and Paul, so good to *see* you." Wearing a short turquoise strapless dress that showed more than a hint of cleavage, Nancy swept into the living room. In her right hand she held high an old-fashioned glass filled with amber liquid and a few ice cubes. "Scotch anyone?" She waved for them to follow her into the den at the far end of the room.

At the sight of Lew, she stopped short. "Oh . . ."

"Mrs. Jarvison," said Lew, extending her hand. "So sorry to barge in on you like this. I'm—"

"I know who you are," said Nancy, her tone blunt. She ignored Lew's hand.

"Yes, well, Dr. Osborne was hoping you wouldn't mind my coming along," said Lew with an ingratiating smile. "Mr. Barber and I are expecting to hear from the Wausau Crime Lab this evening—the results of the autopsy on his son. In the event they need input from one or the other of us I thought this the easiest way to coordinate sharing the information."

"Fine," said Nancy, turning away. "I'll have Cynthia set an extra place. You can get yourself a drink in the den. Jake, a glass of wine or a cocktail?" Nancy was onto Jake Barber as if there was no one else in the room.

Lew gave Osborne a slight nod and without a word, they mutually decided to leave Jake to fend for himself.

Walking into the den, Osborne saw a familiar face behind the bar. "Cynthia," he said, "what are you doing here?" Before the petite, dark-haired woman could answer, he pulled Lew forward to introduce her. "Cynthia was one of my patients. Cynthia and her husband and two children for—what—twelve years?"

"At least," said the woman. "You were so kind when Joe died." She looked at Lew and dropping her voice she said, "We owed Dr. Osborne a lot of money. It was right when my husband became ill that I had to have two crowns and you know how much those cost. You know, Dr. Osborne, you never sent me an invoice. One of these days, maybe? I am getting back on my feet financially."

Osborne waved his hand. "Do not worry about that."

He had known at the time of Joe's diagnosis that the family had no health insurance. Joe's illness bankrupted them. It was one of those things that had driven Mary Lee crazy: Osborne's generosity when he knew people could not pay. It was a habit he had picked up from his own father who would take venison, blueberries, and rhubarb preserves in trade from patients short on cash.

But it was a characteristic that had divided Osborne's household. "Paul," his late wife would say through gritted teeth, "that's not your worry—those people owe you. And we have the new kitchen to pay for."

"So, Cynthia, what are you doing here?" asked Osborne.

"Housekeeping for Mr. and Mrs. Jarvison so I can afford to go back to school," said Cynthia as she poured Osborne a ginger ale. "I plan to get an associate degree in business so I can work as an executive assistant. Both my kids have jobs in the cities these days and I'm only forty-two, so I have time." She smiled.

"Good for you," said Osborne.

"Cynthia? Get in here. I need an extra place setting and stop letting that ice drip on the floor, would you?"

"Be right there, Mrs. Jarvison." Cynthia handed Lew a glass of white wine then bent to dab at a few drips on the hardwood floor beneath the bar. She reached for a bar towel and, kneeling, set it over the wet spot as it was obvious the ice bucket was leaking.

"Is she always so pleasant?" asked Lew, bending over to whisper.

Looking up, Cynthia rolled her eyes and whispered back, "Two more weeks and I'll have saved enough to be out of here. It's okay."

Before Cynthia hurried off toward the dining room, Osborne gave her a sympathetic pat on the shoulder. When she had gone, he looked at Lew. "In case you ever think you're having a bad day—"

Before he could finish, Bud appeared in the doorway, a highball glass in one hand. Weaving, he crossed the room to the bar, reached for a bottle of Bushmills whiskey, and topped off his glass. Only then did he notice Lew standing beside Osborne.

Startled, his jaw slackened as his eyes darted from side to side. At first Osborne thought the man was looking for an escape route but Bud caught himself, cleared his throat, and said, "Well, well, so Doc here took my advice after all."

"Not sure what you mean by that," said Osborne, "but I don't believe you've met Lewellyn Ferris, Bud. I was hoping you and Nancy wouldn't mind as Jake and Chief Ferris learned a short time ago that they might have to take care of some—"

"No, I have not yet had the pleasure," said Bud, his tongue thick as he interrupted Osborne.

Lew threw Osborne a quick glance: someone was over-served. A little too over-served in Osborne's opinion. He decided to do his best to find a polite way to exit the dinner party as soon as possible. He had been around Bud drunk one too many times. It was never a pleasant experience.

But rushing through dinner did not prove to be easy. Nancy continued to schmooze Jake through the dinner while downing glass after glass of red wine. The more she drank, the louder her insistence that she understood his loss and the farther away Jake moved his chair.

After one too many maudlin remarks about their late sons, Jake said in a calm, authoritative tone, "Nancy, I prefer we not mention Liam again this evening."

The table went silent. Fortunately it was only a minute or two before Cynthia walked in from the kitchen to remove their plates and serve dessert. Shortly after the chocolate mousse had arrived, Lew got a text message on her cell phone.

"Oh, dear," she said getting up from the table. "I apologize but I'm afraid that Mr. Barber and I better head back to the station. Looks like there is a fax from the crime lab that needs a response this evening if they're to release the body on Monday. I'm so sorry that we have to run off."

"Oh, for chrissake, why don't you just call in?" asked Nancy, her words slurring. "You can't leave yet—right, Bud? We're having nightcaps down on the dock."

"Nancy, I would love to stay," said Jake, "but Chief Ferris is right. There may be legal issues regarding the release of my son's body and I do not want that delayed any longer. I appreciate your gracious hospitality this evening but—"

"And I have to be at the hospital to check on my grandson," said Osborne.

"That's okay, all of you go," said Bud, lurching out of his chair. "How'sss that grandson of yours doing?" He was so sloshed it took Osborne a moment to figure out what he'd said.

"Much better," said Osborne. "Cody is still in isolation but he's awake and his color is improving. He may be released in the next day or two."

As the three of them walked down the long, winding drive past the four-car garage to where Osborne had parked his car, Jake checked back over his shoulder to be sure he wouldn't be heard before saying, "Please, God, save me from that woman."

Lew chuckled. "She sure has you in her sights."

Jake shook his head. "This was one long night—felt like a rainy day in Cleveland."

"Hold up, you two," said Osborne as they neared the car. "Lew, before we leave, let's take that side path down toward the water and show Jake the view from the bluff."

Chapter Twenty-Five

"Bud Jarvison's grandfather built his manor on the highest point of this bluff overlooking Lake Tomahawk," said Osborne as Lew and Jake followed him along a well-worn path running along a fence behind the Jarvison's garage. "That was back in the late 1800s.

"Years later , he donated a section of his lake frontage for use as a public boat landing, which earned him a tax break that was significant in those days. So this path, which runs along Bud and Nancy's property for a hundred yards or so, takes us to a scenic outlook. Great spot for a picnic."

"What a magnificent view," said Jake as they reached the crest of the bluff and looked out over the lake. The three of them stood in awed silence as a full moon sent daggers of light across the black water. A zillion stars scattered jewels on the waves. On the landing down below, a pickup was backing a boat trailer into the water. The night air was so clear that they could hear the fishermen planning where to stop for beers after securing their boat on the trailer.

"This path and all the land five miles to the north of us belongs to the town," said Osborne, gazing at the serene setting before them as he put an arm around Lew's shoulders. "In the summertime thousands of people use the public access here—fishermen, pleasure boats, kayakers, you name it."

"By the way, Chief Ferris, you didn't really have a text saying there's a fax from the crime lab back at the station, did you?" asked Jake.

"I fibbed," said Lew, "but I thought it wise to leave the party under any pretenses."

"Thank you," said Jake. "Thank you very much."

A new set of voices drifted toward them in the night air. "Do you have any idea how good it feels to be around a *smart* man for a change? I sure as hell don't think Jake Barber is a million bucks in debt. Do you?" Nancy's words slurred one into the other as she hammered on her husband.

A low grunt could be heard: Bud's response.

Eyes wide, Lew, Jake, and Osborne looked at one another. They stood frozen in place, hoping they were out of sight of the happy couple.

"They must be on their dock having that nightcap," said Osborne in a whisper.

"You mean *nightcaps*," said Jake.

"Guess we better head back to the car before they notice we haven't left yet," said Lew softly.

"I doubt they can see straight," said Jake as the three of them tiptoed along the path.

"Will you shut the hell up? I'm working on it." That was Bud.

"Work? You don't work. You've never worked. You just sit around in that stupid office of yours and pretend you're your old man." Nancy was quiet for a moment then she said, "I take that back. You did work. You worked really hard on taking a $30 million fortune and blowing it all in the stock market. I know you had to work goddamn hard to accomplish *that*."

A slurping sound—or was it spitting? Osborne wasn't sure. They were nearly to the car now.

"Yes, you brilliant man. A $30 million fortune and now, you dumb ass, we're $1 million in debt. Hell, we can't even sell this house—how the hell many mortgages do you have on it? Stop, where are you going?"

"My boat," slurred Bud, "only place where I can get away from you." A loud thump followed.

"Sounds like he fell in the boat," whispered Jake.

"Hey, hold up for a second, you two," said Lew in a soft voice. "Let's be sure he doesn't take the boat out. He's in no condition—I'll have to call in if he does."

They waited but there was only the sound of a clinking glass. Then someone vomited.

Osborne helped Lew in on the passenger side while Jake slid onto the backseat and tried to close the car door quietly. No one breathed until they were on the highway.

"Think marriage counseling would help?" asked Jake from the backseat, and they all burst into laughter.

"Stop it now," said Lew, "we're being mean." And she laughed again.

Before getting out of the car at the entrance to the inn, Jake said, "Tomorrow is Sunday. Chief, if you have the day off, would you like that lesson on tenkara fly-fishing?"

"You know, that is a great idea. Let me text our friend, Bruce. He won't want to miss that. If he doesn't mind driving up tomorrow, that will make it easy for us to get an early start on Monday. He'll never forgive me if he doesn't get the lesson too."

"And me? What about me?" Osborne did his best to sound hurt.

"The more the merrier," said Jake, holding the car door open. "By all means, Doc, I know you need to help with your grandson but we'll just be a couple hours or so. Once you know when you need to be at the hospital, give me a call. We'll work around your schedule."

He stepped out of the car, paused, then got back in. He shut the door. "Something is bothering me. Something I saw at the Jarvison's tonight." He was quiet for moment then said, "Chief Ferris, what I saw is hardly proof of anything but I have to mention it."

"Go right ahead, Jake," said Lew.

"You two were talking to that woman behind the bar when Nancy gave me a grand tour of their place. When we were in Bud's study, I saw a small wooden box on the mantel over the fireplace. A box almost identical to the one my son used to carry his trout flies. Jarvison's got wood carvings all around the room but that box stands out."

Lew turned around to stare at Jake. "That doesn't make sense."

"No, of course it doesn't. I asked her about it and she had no idea where it came from. She did comment that she hadn't noticed it before."

"They have a lot of art that Bud inherited from his father and grandfather. The family's been known for their collections of antique duck decoys and fishing lures," said Osborne.

"Well . . . could be there are a lot of small boxes like that around."

"Would there be an identifying mark of some kind on your son's box?" asked Lew.

"I think so. I believe there is a red seal on the bottom."

"And did you check to see if—"

"No. I didn't think to do that until later. I should have—it would have made me feel better." Sadness filled Jake's voice.

"I'm sorry, Jake. I'm so sorry for everything." Lew's voice trembled.

Jake reached across the car seat to grasp her hand and squeeze. "I know. And I thank you both. Just a break like this evening helps. Tomorrow in the river—that will be good." He whispered, "Good night."

• • •

Lew's last thought that night as she lay next to Osborne in the dark, listening to the hoot of a marauding owl, was to wonder— along with the FBI—where Bud was getting all that cash. Selling family heirlooms on eBay?

Chapter Twenty-Six

"I called one of the kayakers who found Peter Corbin to find out where they put in their kayaks," said Lew as she drove her pickup along a forest road that wound through the national forest. "I want to avoid the area where we found Liam because Ray is still searching that location. He thought he could put in another four or five hours today but he said it's been rough going through the swamps along there."

"So no traces of the shooter yet?" asked Jake.

Jake, Bruce, Osborne, and Lew had squeezed themselves into the little truck that Lew used for fishing.

"It's designed to fit four," she had said hopefully.

"Yeah? Four munchkins," said Bruce, tucking his knees up under his chin. "I think Mr. Barber here is going to have me arrested for molesting him."

"Hey, to answer Jake's question a minute ago," said Lew, "Ray's found nothing significant. But given that it's been months since hunting season and we haven't had rain for ten days, he's confident that when and if he comes across signs of a person or people having been back in there, they may well be just who we're looking for. No other reason for them to be there."

"Ah ha!" she said, squealing her tires as she yanked the truck into a small clearing to the left of the road. "Look at *that*." Lew pointed over a cluster of sumac to a glimmer of blue. "The river is right here. Everybody out."

Before they pushed through the brush to head down a slope to the river's edge, Lew lowered the tailgate. She handed out the waders they had stuffed in there along with Jake's tenkara rods. While they were pulling on their waders, Lew set four brown paper bags on the open tailgate.

"If anyone gets hungry," she said as she struggled into her own waders, "those lunch bags are filled with treats. You get a peanut butter sandwich, a little cheese and crackers, and the first raspberries of the summer. But no eating until after class—right, teach?" She grinned at Jake.

"Right you are," he said with a smile. He was the happiest Osborne had seen him since they first met. Though his face was lined with the vestiges of grief, he appeared to be at peace for the moment.

"Oh, and there's one more bag here—chocolate chip cookies. Baked 'em this morning." On that happy note they trudged down to the river.

As they neared the river's edge, Jake dropped back to whisper to Osborne, "Lewellyn certainly is one Swiss Army knife of a woman, isn't she?" He sounded so admiring that Osborne gave him a sharp look.

"Tenkara is fly-fishing in the most traditional sense," said Jake as he waded into the water a few feet from shore. Holding a rod in his hands, he gestured as he spoke. "Your rod casts the line with a fly at the end that drifts but the tenkara rod is different from a traditional fly rod—it's fourteen feet long, you tie the line at the end, add three feet of tippet and a dry fly. No reel. That's the major difference from the fly-fishing you've done in the past: *no reel.*

"Chief Ferris, this is Liam's rod so you take this one," he said, handing Lew one of the two rods he had carried down to the water. "You've got 5X tippet on there and I tied on a Royal Wulff, which is the trout fly I prefer."

"It's 'Lew' today, Jake," said Lew. "I'm off the clock."

"Lew it is," said Jake with a wide smile.

A little too wide, thought Osborne.

"Bruce and Doc," Jake continued, "you two will take turns with my rod. Same line length, about twelve feet. The line is more like a leader than a line—it's not as heavy as the traditional fly line."

"But it's pink," said Bruce, sounding chagrined. "Does it have to be pink? And what test is it?"

"Don't mind Bruce," said Lew from where she had waded knee-deep in the river. "He always gets his shorts tangled in too much detail."

"I'm a Type-A techie, I can't help it," said Bruce.

"Fifteen-pound-test fluorocarbon to answer your question, Bruce," said Jake. "But Lew has a point. Tenkara fly-fishing is less about technique than adventure."

"Looks to me like you're pretty limited in how far you can cast," said Osborne, watching Bruce flick the Royal Wulff tied at the end of their tenkara rod.

"True," said Jake. "But you make up for that in presentation. Watch me cast . . . see how little line is on the water? No drag. Just so you know, there are many fly-fishermen who don't like tenkara," said Jake. "To be fair, a tenkara purist doesn't worry about matching the hatch or owning thousands of trout flies. All that matters is presentation.

"Plus you don't have much gear to carry. That's what my son loved about it. He would put his fly box with two trout flies in one pocket of his fishing vest, carry the telescoped rod in one hand, and the only other thing he might need were waders. Half the time you don't need waders because you're fishing a narrow stream from the bank. Oh, and lunch—especially if Lew Ferris has made it." Again a wide smile that Osborne was beginning to question.

"So let's say that I like this tenkara style of fishing," said Bruce, "what the heck can I do about it? If I can't buy the rod and correct line here in the U.S. am I supposed to drive down to Chicago and borrow yours?"

"Excellent point," said Jake. "I'm glad you brought that up, Bruce. Turns out that even though very few people in this country had ever heard of tenkara before 2009, it has since taken on a cult status among quite a few devotees—including some people so dedicated that they learned Japanese so they can use tenkara's native tongue when they're fishing.

"But to answer your question, you can now buy tenkara rods, lines, and accessories at places like Orvis and Temple Fork Outfitters. When it comes to the tenkara flies, the classic Japanese tenkara fly is almost identical to one of our soft-hackle wet flies. Personally I like to use a Humpy or a Royal Wulff because they entice a trout just as well as any."

"Ah," said Bruce, "now I'm in trouble. Not like I don't own enough fly rods already—but, hey, life is too short not to buy one more, right?"

The Sunday morning could not be finer. The sun was bright and the water a cerulean blue plucked from the sky. The grasses, wild flowers, pines, and stands of birch were a summer medley of buttery yellows and vibrant greens sparked with flashes of brilliant birch white. Burbling riffles in the Pine River lent soft harmonies to the vista surrounding them.

After waiting to see that each of his students felt comfortable with their casts, Jake wandered up the river to where it narrowed, flowing between large boulders lining the riverbank. Lew followed behind Jake, staying back a ways and casting as she went, while Bruce sat on a stump watching Osborne practice.

At the sight of a wide pool behind a boulder ten feet away, Lew decided this would be her spot. She lifted her right arm, tenkara rod held high, and cast with the same motion as her roll cast. The trout fly wobbled then dropped close to her feet. *Okay, that didn't work very well*, she thought as she raised her arm again. This time, she used the roll cast motion again, only to have the dry fly flop just a few feet farther out.

Lew stood still for a long moment trying to visualize the instructions Jake had given them. Maybe tenkara style just wasn't for her—why struggle when she knew she was an expert fly caster in the traditional mode? She decided to relax and just flick the damn thing sideways. To her surprise, the trout fly flew across the water to land just shy of the far bank. She watched it float as lightly as a dragonfly before flicking it again. And again. Each time the trout fly landed like an angel descending from heaven. Lew smiled, she was mesmerized. Okay, if this was what Jake called "the Zen of fly-fishing," she could be all about Zen.

Downstream from Lew, Osborne handed the tenkara rod over to Bruce and stepped back to watch him try. The sound of someone moving against the current caused him to look upstream past Lew.

Fifty yards ahead of Lew he watched as Jake leaned against a large boulder and dropped his head. His shoulders shook and Osborne sensed his shirt would be wet with tears. How could he not feel a sweep of anguish that his son had to die even if it was in a beautiful place where sunlight sparkled like diamonds cast across the water?

Lew approached the grieving father and laid an arm across his shoulders. Now Osborne felt a definite pang of envy. Lew had to feel a bond of loss with Jake. Add to that Jake's impressive career, his expertise in the trout stream, the reality that he was a nice-looking man, a good man. And not only that, he was likely just a year or two older than Lew. She must be attracted to him.

"Hey, speaking of lunch," said Bruce, leaping up from the stump. "I'm hungry."

"Wait for us," said Lew.

As she and Jake waded side by side, Jake laid an arm across Lew's shoulders while she stepped into the curve of his tall frame to wrap one arm around his waist. Osborne saw her give Jake a quick hug before the four of them set their rods on the riverbank and started up toward the truck.

Just as they got to where they could see over the sumac, Osborne thrust both hands out saying, "Whoa, stop."

At the tailgate, paper sacks ripped apart, were two four-legged creatures, their tawny coats and lupine bodies unmistakable in the bright sunlight: wolves. Forelegs braced on the tailgate, one was nose-deep in one of the lunch bags. The other was scarfing the contents of the other bags, which were strewn on the ground under the truck.

No one had the urge to interfere. Slowly, slowly the four fishermen backed away before scrambling down to the riverbank.

"How far is it to the Pine Tree Diner?" asked Bruce, brushy eyebrows bobbing up and down with glee. "Man, this will be one good story for the guys in the lab. Jeez Louise."

Chapter Twenty-Seven

The parking area of the Pine Tree Diner was packed with a late Sunday breakfast crowd, forcing Lew to park on the road. As they approached the battered screen door entrance, her cell phone rang.

"Chief Ferris—where are you?"

The tension in Ray's voice stopped Lew. She spun away from the door. Bruce and Osborne paused beside her. Jake stood back, waiting.

"What's wrong? Are you safe?"

"Yes, I'm safe. Surprised as hell but, yeah, I am safe."

"What's the problem?" Osborne watched Lew's face as she listened.

She covered the phone and leaned sideways to whisper to Osborne, "Ray talking fast is never a good sign."

"A little over two hours ago, I stumbled on a massive marijuana farm not 500 yards from where we found Liam Barber. *Acres of the shit!* Pardon my language. We are so damn lucky they didn't shoot us—or one of the Wausau boys. Gotta tell you, do not let anyone go within a ten-mile radius of that section until you've got reinforcements, Chief. You won't believe the size of the operation and they are armed."

"Slow down, will you? I've got Bruce and Doc right here. Is it okay for you to talk right now?" Lew switched her cell on to speaker so Bruce and Osborne could hear.

"Sure, I just got out of there. I'm in my truck. I can talk fine. I was walking north along the Pine River from where we found Liam's body when I saw what looked like an illegal dumpsite. There was all kinds of trash thrown in the water—plastic garbage bags, empty Gatorade jugs, a deer carcass, clothing, beer cans, you name it. I was thinking some squatter was living back in those woods so I walked over to the dump—and fell in."

"You *fell in?*"

"Kind of. Only it was no dump. Under all the logs and branches was a black tarp and under that I found generators and water pumps. Quite the operation, too. The water pumps are linked to a full-scale irrigation system.

"I'm lucky no one was around—this was before six this morning. Before I left, I was able to get a good look at the size of the place. It runs from the river back into the woods pretty deep. I hid behind bushes along the outskirts and kept going until I spotted some sheds they got set up. There's a good-sized barn that looks like the kind you cure tobacco in and a greenhouse. I got good photos of the buildings. Like I said, this is quite the operation.

"The whole area has been clear cut and the plants look real healthy. Then around seven, people started moving. That's when I saw two dudes carrying rifles with telescopic lenses. I could hear 'em talking and they have to be from south of the border. My high school Spanish isn't great but I know it when I hear it."

"Dogs?" asked Lew.

"No dogs. Trust me, if they'd had dogs, I wouldn't have got close to the place. But no dogs and if they ever had dogs I'll bet you the wolves got 'em."

"Any idea how many people are out there?"

"I saw seven—five men and two women. Also, I counted five vehicles—a couple older model sedans, two pickups, and a good-sized utility truck. I'm betting they use those for deliveries."

"Okay, Ray, we'll grab a bite to go and meet you back in town. I have to get Sheriff Moore in on this."

"Wait, Chief. One more thing: there is only one road going in to this weed farm, okay? No other access so far as I can tell unless you take the river. I've got GPS coordinates for the road as well as the parameters of the growing operation but I think you'll be *real* interested in a certain jabone who drove by just as I was leaving . . . a white guy in a big red SUV . . . a white guy named . . . Bud."

Osborne swore he could hear Ray licking his lips before he said, "Bud . . . Jarvison."

"Did he see you?" asked Lew.

"I don't think so. My truck was parked back in the clearing where we started our search the other day. I followed him just far enough to see him turn down that dirt road I'm telling you about."

Chapter Twenty-Eight

An hour later, after dropping Jake off at the inn, a group of six gathered around the conference table in Lew's office: Doc, Lew, Ray, Bruce, Garry Moore, and Alan Strickland.

"I am sorry to ruin your Sunday afternoon, boys, but we have a dangerous situation in our backyard. Before I start, Garry and Bruce, have you met Alan Strickland? He's with the FBI and working a bank fraud tip that the late Peter Corbin sent them a couple months ago. Alan, Garry is our county sheriff and Bruce is with the Wausau Crime Lab."

The three men nodded at one another.

"Alan is here because the FBI's regional office was tipped that Bud Jarvison has been making cash deposits structured to come in just below the ten grand limit that triggers SARs—Suspicious Activity Reports. I invited Alan to this meeting because it involves Mr. Jarvison."

Over the next twenty minutes Lew described Ray's findings, including the sighting of Bud Jarvison driving in the direction of the marijuana plantation. She had blown up a map of the area on which Ray had pinpointed the GPS coordinates of the marijuana-growing site and the single access route.

"Over here," said Lew, pointing to a red X, "is the riverbank where we found the body of the young researcher, Liam Barber. I've had confirmation from the Wausau Crime Lab that he died from a bullet to the head. Based on Ray's observations, it could have come from one of the men guarding the marijuana operation. Ray took a photo of one man carrying a rifle with a telescopic lens, which means it is capable of shooting long distances.

"Over here," she said, pointing to another red X, "is the approximate location on the river where we found the remains of Peter Corbin who disappeared last February. If I draw a line from the Corbin site to the Barber site and to the coordinates of the road leading in to the pot plantation, we get a triangle." Lew drew the lines with a pencil then stepped back. "My hunch is both victims were shot by guards to prevent them from getting within sight of the marijuana-growing area."

"But Corbin died in the winter," said Garry. "Do you think the drug cartel had people out there in the dead of winter? Certainly not growing anything."

Lew laid a photo of a greenhouse on the table. "Ray shot this with a zoom lens. Could be they have heated greenhouses. More likely, they have their couriers delivering the pot grown and cured over the summer.

"We all know that Milwaukee, Minneapolis, Madison—even Rhinelander—are major markets for controlled substances. If one plant can produce one pound of marijuana and the street value of that one pound is $2,500, I doubt they stop dealing because the weather changes. Right now, in Loon Lake alone, we are seeing a significant increase in the number of young people being arrested for possession of marijuana. This is a marked change from this time last year and I am willing to bet we're looking at the source right in our backyard."

"I agree with Chief Ferris," said Garry. "We're seeing the problem escalating county-wide."

"Let's not waste time, Chief Ferris. You gotta go in with a SWAT team," said Alan. "ASAP."

"He's probably right," said Garry reluctantly. "What I don't like is these cartel guys are so well protected by trees that SWAT team or not—and, Alan, I head up the SWAT team for our five-county region—my people are going to be at risk. Grave risk. We need to strategize.

"For the record, I am not taking any dogs in there. You think the Mexican cartel is dangerous? Try sending an expensive, well-trained K-9 dog into a wolf rendezvous site right when the packs are at the height of guarding their pups. No way am I sacrificing my dogs."

"What's this about a wolf rendezvous site?" asked Alan. "Never heard the term before."

"It's where a wolf pack keeps the young pups who have been weaned but are not mature enough to hunt," said Garry. "The packs are very territorial so any dog that is unfortunate enough to wander into the area is considered a threat—or dinner—and is killed by the pack. I know four bear hunters out training their dogs who have had good dogs killed—'depredated' is the term used by the DNR.

"This particular region in the Nicolet National Forest happens to fall between three or four territories so it's uncertain which of three packs have been killing the dogs. But as a result of the depredations the DNR has established a four-mile buffer around there. In other words, you do not go in there with a dog and, frankly, this time of year when the pups are active and the pack is guarding them—I would not send one of my children in there."

"How many wolves are you talking about?" asked Alan. "Hundreds? Thousands?"

"Oh, gosh, no," said Garry. "There will be the alpha male and alpha female, which are the only pack members allowed to mate, and the female will have on average four to six pups. The greater question that I cannot answer is how many adult wolves are in the pack plus the number of pups. I don't know if different packs allow their pups to be together in the one rendezvous site. So my best guess is twenty to thirty wolves counting adults and pups.

Maybe not that many but they are vicious killers so numbers are less critical than—"

From the back of the room, Ray interrupted, "Excuse me, Sheriff Moore. Run that by me again about the wolf pups."

"This time of year is when the packs are actively patrolling that specific area to protect their pups," said Garry. "Just this week the USDA Wildlife Services reported that twenty hunting dogs have been killed since spring."

"If . . . that is the case," said Ray, "I have a thought."

As Ray spoke, Osborne saw the sheriff lean forward in his chair. Garry was well aware of Ray's talents when it came to understanding wildlife. Alan, on the other hand, looked off with a shrug as if his time was being wasted.

"Go ahead, Ray," said Lew.

"Consider . . . a wolf howl box," said Ray. "We borrow a couple from the University Wildlife Research Unit . . . three should do the trick. They've been using them to track wolves . . . because the wolves are fooled into thinking the howls they hear are from real wolves . . . and they respond.

"We set up the howl boxes so the pot growers think they're surrounded . . . that they're being attacked by howling wolves." Ray grinned. "So you *scare* 'em out . . . they aren't likely to run on foot . . . and . . . there is only one road out."

"I don't get it," said Alan, shaking his head.

"Well, sir, I am afraid of wolves, aren't you?" asked Ray.

"Don't know. Never been around one," said Alan. A soft chuckle went around the room.

Sheriff Moore raised his hand. "Everyone, if I were in a situation confronting an alpha female wolf who felt threatened or that her pups were threatened by me I would be very afraid of that wolf. Just like Ray here. But Ray, I'm not sure where you are going with this."

"I think . . ." Ray looked up at the ceiling as he talked, "if I were a guy from Mexico . . . or California . . . forced to live in the deep woods with wolves all around me . . . well, I would not be happy. And if . . ." said Ray, raising the index finger on his right hand while making eye contact one at a time with everyone sitting around the table, "if . . . one dark night . . . I heard a whole bunch of 'em howling right outside my bedroom . . . well . . ."

"I would leap in my car and get the hell out of there," said Lew with a grin.

"They're sure not going to run deeper into the woods," said Bruce. "I like this idea—but I'm a scientist, not law enforcement. What do you guys think?" Bruce glanced around the room.

"So you're saying we should use the sound of howling wolves to scare the bejesus out of these guys. And when they come hell-bent out of there, we're ready for 'em? I like it," said Garry. He looked at Lew. "I'll put out a call for backup from my five-county region—we'll be armed and ready without having to go in shooting and risking lives."

"Might work," said Ray. "And if it doesn't . . . you've still got your SWAT team."

"Okay, okay," said Lew, "but first, Ray, how do the howl boxes work? Do we mount them on vehicles with loudspeakers and—"

"Oh no." Ray got to his feet and walked up to the conference table. "A wolf howl box is the size of a laptop," he said, demonstrating with his hands as he spoke. "Each box weighs less than ten pounds . . . and runs on batteries. It's got a microphone and speakers built in . . . so that it can broadcast the howls . . . and record the wolves that respond.

"The howl box was originally developed by wildlife researchers in Montana and it's amazingly simple in concept . . . very loosely based on the audio tools used in researching birds . . . the howl boxes are digitally programmed to perform different types of howls . . . and to store the responses from wolves in the wilderness . . . who are fooled into thinking they're howling back at their friends and enemies. Operating a howl box is easy as pie . . . I know where we can get one for sure. Want me to?"

"Please," said Lew.

Ray left the room to use his cell phone outside for a better connection. Within five minutes he was back. "Got three . . . told my buddy who works with the Wildlife Services what we need 'em for . . . he's going to refresh the batteries and deliver them in an hour or so . . . is that okay? I promised to take him out for trophy muskie next week . . . let's pray the big girls are biting."

"So when do we do this?" asked Alan. "Tomorrow night?"

"Tonight," said Lew. "It's four o'clock right now—how 'bout we plan for two in the morning?"

"You don't have time to organize," said Alan.

"Yes we do," said Garry. "Chief Ferris is right. We do it tonight."

"You people are crazy," said Alan. "It's Sunday, your officers are trying to have a weekend with family."

"That is why we do it tonight," said Lew. "On Sunday nights everyone in the entire United States lets down their guard. They don't lock their doors or turn on their security systems. We have more break-ins on Sunday than any other day of the week. Pot growers may be criminals but they're human and they enjoy their Sundays, too. We move tonight."

Chapter Twenty-Nine

Osborne listened as Lew and Garry outlined the plan for the evening. Police and sheriffs' deputies from Loon Lake, Oneida, and four surrounding counties would meet at the Pine Tree Diner at midnight. One at a time over the next ninety minutes, the patrol cars would follow one another, lights off, to park along a forest road that was a quarter-mile from the dirt road leading into the marijuana-growing operation.

"Any cars coming along that forest road after midnight will be stopped," said Lew. "We'll put up a roadblock and drivers will be told there has been a fatal accident and the road is temporarily closed. We will also work with the cell service providers for this region to take down cell service—we don't need anyone texting, e-mailing, or phoning for those three hours.

"Ray, you and Doc will ride with me. We'll go in first to give Ray time to set up the howl boxes. Doc, you'll stay with me and be ready to assist Ray with extra batteries, etc. Before we drive out there this evening, let's do a test run with the boxes and the remotes to be sure everything is in working order."

Osborne left the meeting and hurried home to feed the dog and grab a bite to eat. Then he went back to the hospital. He had promised Erin he would be there by six.

"Good evening, Dr. Osborne," said the receptionist with a wide smile as he walked through the empty waiting room.

He was a little surprised at her good humor. Knocking on the door to Cody's room, he said in a low voice, "Erin, it's me—Dad."

The door opened a crack and Erin peered through. She gave him a wink as she said, "Close your eyes, Dad, and don't open until I say so."

Osborne did as he was told. "Okay, you can come in now." The room was quiet for a change—no machines were humming. "Wait . . . now. Go ahead and open your eyes."

Osborne's jaw dropped.

A curious figure was sitting up on pillows and wearing a stuffed trout on his head and a toothy smile on his face. "Hi, Grandpa," said Cody. "I'm all well."

"*Almost* all well," said Erin at the look of surprise on Osborne's face. "Treating the strep in his bloodstream turned the corner for whatever strange medical reason. No fever, no headache since lunchtime." She bent over to hug her son. "We have our little Cody back. And Dad," she exhaled happily, "they think he can go home tomorrow."

Osborne felt the tension flow out of his body for the first time in days. "What a relief. What an amazing relief."

"To put it mildly," said his daughter with a smile. "They plan on moving him out of isolation tomorrow morning after one more round of tests. The only disappointment is that none of these wonderful gifts he got can go home. It's the rule for anyone who has been treated in one of the isolation wards."

"Not even the *Lunkers* book or his hat from Ray?"

"No, sorry. Hospital's pretty firm on that. Too bad, huh."

"Well, sport," said Osborne, "we'll just have to buy a new book and I'm sure Ray can find you another hat."

"No, Grandpa, Ray told me this hat is the only one in the whole wide world." Cody appeared on the edge of tears.

"We'll see about that, Cody. Can we worry about it tomorrow?" asked his mother.

The little guy sniffed as he whispered, "Okay."

"Crying or not, it's great to have you awake and alert, little guy," said Osborne.

Later that evening, before leaving the house to meet Ray and Lew, Osborne, hoping to order another copy of *Lunkers*, checked Amazon. No luck. It was out of print and the cheapest copy on eBay was $148.00—a lot of money for a "used paperback with curling pages."

Hmm. Maybe one of his McDonald's buddies might have a copy. He'd check around.

Chapter Thirty

Sitting inside Lew's cruiser, Osborne watched as the squad cars flowed in and out of the parking lot at the Pine Tree Diner. As soon as they arrived they were assigned a place to park along the forest road and told to wait for the signal to leave their vehicles on foot and meet near the entrance to the dirt road leading to the marijuana farm. Two police vans from nearby towns were to be positioned as barriers closing off the forest road in both directions.

"All we need now is to flush those razzbonyas out of there," said Ray from the backseat.

"Ready?" asked Lew, glancing back at Ray.

"Ready as the raindrops, Chief."

"Me, too," said Osborne, looking down at his watch. It was ten to one. Ray had figured it would take him forty minutes to walk in and set up the wolf howl boxes.

"What would we do without GPS coordinates?" asked Lew rhetorically as she drove slowly past the unmarked dirt road.

"That plus I compared the *Gazetteer* map with the latest plat book from the county so I got a good idea just where I want to set these howl boxes," said Ray.

"And a flashlight? You need a flashlight in case it's tough going back in there," said Osborne.

"No flashlight, Doc. Too much weight. I got enough to handle and the forecast is for clear skies. I'll be able to see fine."

"Are you sure? I've got a pocket-size one you can use." Ray's grunt answered that offer.

"Pull over right here," said Ray when they were about fifty yards from the road.

Osborne climbed out of the car to help Ray unload the three howl boxes. Once his eyes adjusted to the dark, the glow from the waning gibbous moon made it easy to see without using a flashlight.

"All right, Ray, you're on. Please be careful," said Lew. "You can abort at any time if you sense something isn't right. Remember we've got the SWAT team to fall back on."

"I hear you, Chief. But right now, it all looks good. With the moonlight and the fact I'll be moving downwind, I should be fine. No way will they be able to hear me. If they do, they'll think I'm a critter."

"Good," said Lew. "I don't want you shot before two o'clock—or after."

Lew and Doc leaned against the cruiser, watching as Ray headed into the forest, a box in each hand and the third tucked into a backpack slung over one shoulder.

"I'm worried that's too much for him to carry," said Lew.

"He doesn't seem to have a problem with the weight," said Osborne. "I worry he's going to make noise and alert those guards with their telescopic lens. I worry they have night vision goggles. And I worry he won't be able to see where the hell he's going."

"Doc, you made the offer," said Lew, looking around. "He's okay. My eyes have adjusted and I can see fine."

"I guess you're right," said Osborne, surprised to find how anxious he was feeling.

Lew nodded. "This aspen is good cover," she whispered, trying to assure both of them.

They waited in silence. Every few minutes they could hear the faint sound of tires as one squad car after another found its way to the forest road. The roadblock had gone up at one A.M. as planned. At twenty after one, the two police vans pulled up behind Lew's cruiser.

"Sheriff Moore?" Lew whispered through the window of the first one.

"Here," said Garry, his voice a low murmur in the dark. "Have not had a single car come this way in three hours. I think we're good for no alerts so far. The cell service went down half an hour ago. Any sign of movement down that road?"

"No. Ray is in the woods setting up the howl boxes. I expect him out in about twenty minutes, maybe sooner."

Chapter Thirty-One

The early going through the young aspen was frustrating. "Damn it," Ray cursed softly as one pocket of his sweats caught on a branch and yanked him to a stop. He had taken care to forgo his khaki fishing shorts for the worn navy blue sweatshirt and black sweatpants—the better to disappear into the shadows. But he was hot in the humid evening air and the loose clothes kept snagging.

He stopped to adjust his backpack then soldiered on. The aspen gave way to balsam and red pine, much easier going. Off to his right, he could see pinpoints of light, which disappeared after a few minutes. The drug crew turning in for the night? He hoped so. When he felt he had cleared the area where the sheds and living space were located, he stopped to set down the first howl box. He was making sure that it was turned on when he heard footsteps coming his way.

He backed into a stand of pines and stooped low, hoping the feathery needles of a young white pine would hide him. As the steps grew closer, he realized there were two people. When they passed about fifteen feet away, he could hear the low whispers of a woman coaching someone: a mother and child on their way to a latrine.

Oops, thought Ray. He hadn't planned for that. But, of course, there would be no plumbing out here. He stayed quiet until he heard the mother and child pass by again on their way back to their sleeping quarters.

As he waited, barely breathing, he wondered if this was the little boy who had been treated for the deer tick bite and made a mental note to check himself for ticks later. *Lyme disease is hard on the body.* It also struck him that although the law enforcement teams planning to arrest the members of the drug cartel imagined armed men as their targets, the reality was there were women and children here, too. Dealing drugs might be the driving reason for the marijuana plantation but some of these folks were people doing the best they could to survive. At least the woman and child weren't carrying telescopic rifles and they likely had no choice other than to be here tonight: in the wrong place at the wrong time. His final thought before he pushed on was that he hoped the little kid, boy or girl, would be okay.

Another trudge through stands of evergreens, an area that had looked dense enough to hide him when he had scoured the plat book earlier. He was close to what would be the midpoint for positioning the second howl box when his right foot slipped and he went down into waist-deep water, managing at the last minute to hoist the box in his left arm far enough off to one side to keep it partially on the bank and out of the water. The howl box in the backpack was safe for sure but had the other survived the sudden jarring?

Maybe Osborne was right and he should have brought along a flashlight. But even so he would have stuck it in the backpack, which would have put it out of reach and useless in this situation.

Ray got to his feet, hoping he hadn't stumbled into sewage but there was no odor. The canal was manmade and must be part of the irrigation system. That was a good sign. After climbing out of the canal, he could see ahead that the evergreens gave way to a forest of hardwoods where he hoped to find it much easier going. Could be he was not far from the Pine River where he planned to set the third howl box.

After wringing the water from the sodden legs of his sweatpants, he adjusted the backpack, stepped over the canal, and was hurrying to a small clearing where he could set the second howl box when he tripped. He looked down at a weathered two-by-four half hidden by grasses. Now how did that get here? Looking up he could see the vestiges of an abandoned tree stand some deer hunter had built about twelve feet up and cantilevered over the branches of a good-sized maple. Rickety footholds were nailed at random angles into the trunk of the tree. Even in the dark, Ray could see the stand was so weathered with gaping holes in the platform overhead that it hadn't been used in years.

Kicking aside the two-by-four, he knelt to set up the second howl box. Just like the first one, it had a tiny red light that went on to indicate he had them turned on and ready to receive signals from the remote units back in the trunk of Lew's cruiser.

He knew he had to hurry because the wait in the woods and the fall into the canal had taken more time than he had planned. On the other hand, there was no estimating exactly how long this might take given the trek through woods in the dark, so he decided to slow down to be sure he set the third box up correctly.

He reached a section of swamp that had been indicated on the *Gazetteer* and skirted it to find just the right location where a initial blast from the howl box, given the direction of the night breezes, would be an ideal opener for the evening—slightly distant from the others and very likely a spot the pack itself might howl from on occasion. Yep, this would be just perfect for the last howl box, which was in his backpack. Sitting down to zip open his backpack, Ray had pulled out the box and was leaning forward to position it on top of a tree stump when he glanced up.

That's when he saw the eyes: glowing flame-red against the darkness . . . all around him.

He stood stock-still, a familiar mantra running through his mind: *Wolves have never been known to attack humans.*

It was a mantra from childhood. His father had told him that for the first time right after he had taken Ray deer hunting and they had met a wolf on an old railroad track. Ray would never forget how the wolf, which was about fifty feet away, had stood perfectly still watching them.

"Do not make eye contact," his father had warned. "That can be perceived as a threat. I want you to stand your ground, yell, and wave your arms until he runs off." The wolf did not move. "Okay," his father had said, "that isn't working so now we back away. But don't turn around—we have to try to appear intimidating."

And so father and son had backed away slowly, hollering at the top of their voices. It seemed forever that the wolf stood right where it was, watching. When they reached their car, which was parked at an old rail crossing not far away, and scrambled in, Ray's father had exclaimed so loudly with an uncharacteristic curse that Ray knew he had been terrified.

Ray forced himself to keep working: position the howl box, flip the switch to turn it on, double-check the switch, now stand up. The eyes were still there, knee-high and watching. He couldn't make out any shapes in the dark but he figured they had to be wolf pups. He picked up his backpack and started to back away along the edge of the swamp, keeping the eyes in his peripheral vision yet trying hard not to look directly at them either. Yelling was not an option—not if the routing of the drug cartel was to go as planned. And not to mention that one yowl from him and, whether it be man or beast, he'd be lucky to get out of the Nicolet National Forest alive.

At first, the eyes following him seemed curious. Then more sets of eyes, taller than the early ones, joined the crowd. The eyes seemed to move closer and he half expected to feel a curious snout sniffing at the legs of his wet sweatpants. Twice he thought he heard a low growl but he refused to think about it.

Backing through the woods was more difficult than he had hoped. Twice he stumbled backwards but managed to grab branches and stay upright. The eyes moved in closer. He thought about calling for help on his cell phone, which was in the backpack, but remembered that Lew had arranged for all cell service to go down. That was not an option.

But the thought of his backpack jogged a critical memory—earlier he had shoved a roast beef sub sandwich in there. It was supposed to have been his dinner but the preparations that night had gotten so busy he never got around to eating it. Along with that thought came a vision of the packages of venison chops in his freezer. If only he had those in hand, then he might have a chance. One thing he knew—everyone in the Northwoods knew—was that wolves love deer meat. But he did not have any venison. All he had was one roast beef sandwich. The challenge was how to turn around so he could get it out safely without looking weak and frightened. The roast beef sandwich. It wasn't much but maybe, just maybe . . .

A plan started to take shape in Ray's head but it could work only if he was able to retrace his steps with some accuracy. Continuing to keep the glowing eyes in his peripheral vision, he tried to glance around and see if he was on track, returning the way he had come. At first it seemed impossible to tell where he was going but if he could just turn around and take a good look, he might be able to orient himself.

He was still backing up when his right foot struck something hard. He dared to take a quick look down: ah, the old two-by-four. A few seconds later he felt a sturdy tree trunk against his back. *Okay, let's go for it*, he told himself.

Holding the backpack out in front, he did his best to look past the eyes staring at him as he zipped open the backpack, grabbed the sandwich, and in one motion, ripped off its crisp tissue wrapping.

He flung it forward as hard as he could. He could hear it falling in soft clumps as it came apart in the air.

Yelping and shoving, the pups dove for the prize. The eyes disappeared. Turning around so fast he nearly broke his nose on the tree trunk, Ray grabbed for the footholds and, wobbly though they were, pulled himself up one after the other. He hoped to hell the rusted nails wouldn't pull out. They held, and scrambling he managed to find one toehold after another.

Hauling himself up onto the rotten platform, he crouched on the few wooden planks still there and prayed his weight wouldn't dislodge them. From down below he could hear branches snapping as the pups tussled and yelped, tearing at the clumps of bread and roast beef. For an absurd second, he wondered if they preferred mustard or mayonnaise.

He could see better now and the figures of at least six pups emerged from the shadows. Behind them were taller shadows: the adults. He counted four. Very likely two were the parents—the alpha male and alpha female.

Time stood still as he watched from the tree stand, barely breathing. Maybe he was just not very interesting or maybe a new prey had surfaced somewhere but as quickly as the inquisitive eyes had appeared, they were gone. Still Ray waited. He was ready to wait until dawn if he had to—drug cartel and marijuana trafficking aside. The goal at the moment was to stay alive.

He figured he'd waited at least twenty minutes before he was sure the wolves weren't coming back. Slowly, pausing on each a rung as he went, he lowered himself onto the forest floor. Then he ran.

He flew over the canal then slowed, determined to keep his distance from the latrine, then picked up his pace as he neared the aspens crowding the road where he had left Lew and Doc. A shooting pain in his left eye forced him to stop. Too many shadows. He had run right into the pointed end of spindly young red pine. The pain was so intense that he had to stop, take a deep breath, and place one hand over his eye until he could be sure he wasn't bleeding. He slowed to a cautious walk. Even though he was sure he had to be close to the road, he made himself move with both hands held out in front of him, desperate to keep from damaging his other eye.

Chapter Thirty-Two

Back at the police cruiser, Osborne and Lew waited, the sounds of the forest growing louder as the minutes ticked by: rustlings, owls hooting, the scream of a rabbit losing its head.

Lew began to pace back and forth. "Doc, it's been over an hour. According to Ray's plan, he should have been back twenty minutes ago. Something's happened."

"If anything happened, I think we might have heard it," said Osborne, not mentioning gunshots being one guarantee that Ray's mission had gone bad.

"I'm going in," said Lew. "I know the direction he was headed. I am sure I can use a flashlight without alerting anyone."

"Not a good idea, Lew," said Osborne. "You don't really know where he was going once he disappeared behind these aspen. Let's hold on five more minutes."

"Okay, five minutes. Then I may have to call this operation off."

A whisper of soft footsteps and a tall shadow emerged from the wall of aspen. At first Osborne was as relieved to see his neighbor as he had been at the sight of Cody sitting up in his fish hat earlier. Then he became aware that Ray was staggering.

"What on earth?" Lew spoke first. "What happened? Have you been shot?"

"No, no, it's my eye . . . I ran into a branch. I'll be fine . . . we'll worry about it later."

"Oh, no, we won't," said Osborne. "You need the emergency room—now. I did that once and you have to get it treated tonight, I mean this morning."

"All right," said Ray, "but I don't think that one more half-hour is going to kill me. Let's get this done first . . ."

Just then two figures emerged from the dark in front of Lew's cruiser: Alan Strickland and Ron Hardin, the DEA agent who was working with him.

"Chief Ferris?" asked Alan in a low voice. "What the hell is happening? This operation is almost an hour late by my watch."

"Just a brief setback," said Ray, one hand over his eye.

"What do you mean 'a brief setback'?" asked Alan.

"I said it's nothing," said Ray. "I'm ready to set the howl boxes off right now."

"We have to get him to the hospital," said Lew. "He ran a tree branch into his eye. Just as soon as we've finished here, Doc and I will—"

"That's it. Everything's off," said Alan, making a chopping motion with both hands. "Forget this ridiculous setup."

"Alan," said Lew in a warning whisper, "keep your voice down. Doc is ready to take Ray in for treatment as soon as we've run the operation."

"That's nuts. I'm calling for the SWAT team first thing in the morning."

"Maybe . . ." said Ray, walking to the back of the cruiser where the lid of the trunk was open, ". . . maybe you could calm down and let us give this a try . . . no skin off your nose, right?"

Alan snorted and motioned to his colleague. "Remind me of this conversation in the morning when we're marshaling the troops, will you?"

"I think it's worth a try," said the other man. "Pradt is right— we've got nothing to lose and maybe all we hear are a bunch of howling wolves but I'm in. I want to see this."

"Thank you, Ron," said Lew. "Okay, Doc, Ray, are we ready? I'll flick my lights so Sheriff Moore and his people know we're ready."

She and Osborne stood at the back of the cruiser just behind Ray. The trunk was open and the interior light shone down on the three units used to control the wolf howl boxes. Ray dropped his hand from his eye and leaned over to check the signals on the remotes in front of him. Meanwhile, the two police vans had moved in close to the entrance to the dirt road. Looking around at the officers and deputies on foot, Lew counted twenty-two men and women poised to provide backup.

"If these fellas are all from south of the border . . . think they'll understand English?" asked Ray in a whisper.

"They'll understand a badge and a gun," said Lew. "That's what counts." She checked her watch. "Ready . . . go."

Ray threw the first switch and dialed the volume on the first box to a level three out of ten. "This box is twenty yards below where they're sleeping," he said.

He threw the second switch and dialed the volume to a similar level. "This one is closer to the building . . . and the third box is right in line with the windows . . . it should sound closer than the first two."

Osborne could hear a faint howling. Slowly, steadily Ray turned up the volume on all three boxes. "Yes . . . the wolves are closing in," said Ray with a grim smile.

At level ten, the sound of wolves howling in the dark reverberated through the forest.

They waited.

In less than ten minutes, a utility truck alleging to be the property of Jeselnik Plumbing, Heating, and Excavating barreled up the dirt road. At the sight of the first police van, the driver skidded to a halt. The second van pulled in behind the truck at an angle that made it impossible for the driver to back away.

Searchlights raked the side of the utility truck and two squad cars pulled alongside it.

"This is Sheriff Moore," said a voice over a loudspeaker from one of the two vans. "Come out with your hands up and no one will be hurt."

Not a shot was fired. Out of the van tumbled nine terrified people: five men, two women—one expecting—and two children. Found in the van were two Winchester 30-06 rifles fitted with telescopic lenses and twenty-two Ziploc bags filled with marijuana and marked with addresses or phone numbers for delivery. Hidden under the driver's seat was an envelope containing $12,000 and with the letters "BJ" scrawled in black pen on the front.

• • •

"Ray, Doc, this may turn out to be the biggest drug bust in the history of Loon Lake, maybe even the county," said Lew with a satisfied grin as they drove back into town. "I can't believe that we have the names and addresses of the dealers they were delivering to. By the time Sheriff Moore and I collar those people and track down their customers, we will have shut down one hell of an operation."

"Oh, this goes way beyond the county, Chief," said Ray. "Based on the reaction from Strickland's DEA buddy . . . you and Sheriff Moore may have pulled off . . . one of the biggest drug busts in the state . . . certainly in recent years. You better ask for a raise."

Lew grinned even broader. "Thanks, Ray, but do you know what pleases me most? *No one got hurt.* When I saw those two little kids, all I could think was how bad it might have been if we had gone in with the SWAT team. We wouldn't have known . . ."

"And think of the long-term damage for those children," chimed in Osborne. "What a nightmare for a kid: grown-ups shooting guns, their family members killed. This may not be the best situation for them right now but it's certainly better than witnessing acts of violence."

"Speaking of violence," said Ray, "I haven't had a chance . . . to tell you two what happened to me back in there. First . . . I almost gave us away when I was setting up the first howl box . . . and two people showed up."

"What?" asked Lew. "How did you handle that?"

"I hid back in the trees . . . it was one of the women taking one of the kids to the outhouse . . . a latrine, really. Next . . . I slipped and fell into one of their irrigation canals . . . you know," Ray shook his head, "I still can't believe I didn't let out a sound . . . or drop one of the howl boxes . . . I mean, I went down *wham*."

Lew and Osborne chuckled as he spoke. "Well, you're safe and sound now except for that hole in your eye."

"And that is not even the worst . . . I'm down near the riverbank the other side of the swamp that's back in there . . . when I look around and see all these red eyes . . . staring at me from the dark."

"Oh—the wolf pups?" asked Lew.

"Yeah, first the pups then mom and dad . . . then their cousins and their aunts and uncles . . . I counted ten wolves trying to decide if I smelled good enough to eat."

"So that's what took you so long?"

"You better believe it . . . I tried to remember everything I've ever learned about dealing with wolves . . . because oddly enough I have only ever seen one up close . . . and that was when I was a kid hunting with my old man.

"Keep in mind wolves have been almost extinct around here . . . until the last five years or so. So I was doing all the things you're told to try to appear intimidating . . . which is not easy when you're walking backwards into a pitch-dark forest. At one point I was ready to call for help on my cell . . . when I remembered that you took down cell service."

"Oh, Ray," Lew turned to look at him in the backseat. "You must have been terrified."

"I was. And I don't mind telling anyone I was . . . but I had a sandwich in my backpack that I was able to toss at them . . . and that kept them busy long enough for me to scramble up an old tree stand back in there . . . I was lucky. It was either that or I was going to start howling myself . . . and blow our beautiful plan."

"I was wondering why you were moving so fast that you ran into that branch," said Osborne. "That's not like you, Ray. You're pretty at home in the woods night or day."

"Yep, that's what it was all about . . . I don't think I've run that fast since Bobby Enderle chased me home . . . saying he was going to beat me up. That was in third grade . . . and I ran faster 'n that tonight."

"Lew was ready to go in after you," said Osborne. "She had a hunch something had gone wrong."

"Speaking of hunches, Ray," said Lew, "this idea of yours to use the wolf howl boxes was excellent. I'll see that you get a bonus for tonight's work. Mind if I share some of the details—like your episode with the wolf pups? I think our city council would enjoy it."

"Yeah, they can enjoy it all they want . . . I'll use that bonus to buy me another sandwich . . . now that I think about it, I am starving."

"We'll get you home soon. But you can be sure that the powers that be will know that it's thanks to you that we can all take pride in a good night's work," said Lew. "That includes all of us—Sheriff Moore's people, even Alan Strickland, though he did his best to put the kibosh on it. So a huge 'thank you' again, Ray. And, look, we're a block from the hospital."

"You're as welcome as the flowers, Chief. Problem is . . . it's four in the morning right now and I'm supposed to be guiding two guys in about two hours . . . think I have a good reason to reschedule?"

"When I drop you off, give me their phone number and I'll call them for you," said Lew. "Then you call me on my cell when you're ready and I'll give you a ride home."

"No, Lew, this has been quite a night for you, too," said Osborne. "I have a better idea. Let's drop Ray off and you take me back to the station for my car. Then I'll come back here and wait for him. If he's got a corneal abrasion like I had, they'll want to be sure the eye is clean and give him advice on how to help it heal."

"You're sure?" asked Lew.

"We're sure," said the two men in unison. "Yeah, my eye is already feeling better," said Ray. "I'll survive."

• • •

Before climbing out of Lew's cruiser, Osborne turned toward her and instead of his usual quick kiss on her lips, he said, "You know, Lew, there's something I've been thinking about a lot lately. I know it's late but I'll feel better if I mention it."

"This doesn't sound good, Doc. Something wrong?"

Osborne paused before he spoke, a bad feeling in his gut. But he forced himself to say, "Well . . . much as I care for you, Lew, we aren't married . . . so if you find yourself attracted to someone else, I'll understand." He held his breath as he waited for the bad news.

"What?" A stunned expression crossed Lew's face. "Where is *this* coming from?"

"Lewellyn, Jake Barber is a fine man, he's successful, he loves to fish, he's much closer to your age, he's—"

"Whoa, Dr. Osborne. Stop right there. Yes, Jake is a wonderful person but so are you." She grinned at him. "You are ever so much more so. *You*, sweetheart, are my best friend . . ."

"I am?" In spite of the early morning hour, the enthusiasm in her voice made Osborne feel wide awake, sixteen, and awkward all over again—and he loved it.

"Now listen, Doc, I have paperwork to finish before I can sleep so I have to kick you out of my car, but will you promise me this is not an issue between us? Promise?" And she leaned forward to give him the kind of kiss he planned to think about until the sun came up.

Osborne drove back to the hospital where Ray was just coming out of an examining room. "You were right, Doc. They said I've scratched the cornea . . . but it'll heal pretty fast. They gave me some drops to use . . . and sleep will help, too."

"Lew called one of your guiding clients a few minutes ago. Afraid she woke him up but he understood. He said they'll stay over an extra day to fish with you. He was pretty impressed when she told him why you've been up all night."

"Great. Say, Doc . . . do me one more favor? Ask Erin to call me and tell me exactly when she's to pick Cody up to come home . . . *exactly when.* I need to know."

Osborne gave him a puzzled look. "Sure. I know she feels bad that they can't take home that hat you gave him. She can barely get him to take it off at bedtime."

Chapter Thirty-Three

Osborne was sound asleep when his cell phone rang at nine the next morning.

"Hello, Dr. Osborne, this is Cynthia and I apologize for taking so long to get back to you. I was away this weekend but I got your message about that little wooden box. Is this a bad time to talk? You sound like I woke you up."

"No, no, this is fine, Cynthia." Osborne checked the time on his alarm clock and was surprised to see how late it was. "I appreciate your call. Did you find the little box that I mentioned?"

"I believe so. It's on the mantel in Mr. Jarvison's study and I turned it over like you asked. There is a mark in red ink on the bottom. Is that what you were wondering about?"

"Yes. Thank you."

"The Jarvisons are out this morning if you want to stop by and I'll show it to you. Mrs. Jarvison won't be back until ten and Mr. Jarvison is golfing."

Osborne thought that over. "No, thank you, Cynthia, I don't want to get you in trouble. If you don't mind keeping an eye on that box though, I'll talk to Bud about it one of these days."

After saying goodbye, Osborne leaned back against his pillow thinking, *So Bud Jarvison has the wooden fly box that belonged to Liam Barber. That's curious.*

• • •

It was late morning when Nancy Jarvison got home from her workout with her personal trainer. The fitness center was in Rhinelander but she didn't mind the drive. She had to leave before Bud was up and the early morning sessions gave her an opportunity to avoid him, which she appreciated more and more these days.

When he hadn't returned from golfing by four that afternoon, she started to wonder. Was he still at the country club bar or hanging out with that woman the nurse's aides had mentioned? Bud's drinking had grown so out of control in the last couple years that she couldn't count how many times he had blacked out and had to be driven home by one of the creeps he had taken to hanging out with—some of those guys could barely speak English. Class was not Bud's long suit these days.

At 6:30—with the pork roast and parsley red potatoes that Cynthia had prepared still warm on the dining room table—there was still no Bud.

All right. This could be it, thought Nancy, grimacing as she tapped her empty wineglass on the table. *Tomorrow I see a divorce lawyer. For what that's worth. The money, most of it anyway, is gone.*

She had only herself to blame—she should have divorced him years ago. At the very least, she should have paid attention to what he was doing with their money, especially after her father's will had stipulated that her inheritance be rolled into the Jarvison trust.

Thank you, Dad, for trusting my intelligence, thought Nancy as she refilled her glass with chardonnay. She was at least as smart, if not smarter, than Bud. She would never have invested $6 million in a high-tech start-up that went bust after two years—all because it was the brainchild of the son of one of Bud's stupid college buddies. The lawsuits on that venture alone cost another couple million.

And then he goes and puts $30 million in the hands of his fraternity brother, the investment broker running one of the biggest Ponzi schemes in the Midwest. Granted, a lot Bud's friends lost money on that one, too. And she wasn't the only wife ignorant of what the not-so-smart boys were doing.

So if she did divorce Bud, what was left? As of a week ago, the banker managing the family trust said they had 150 grand in stocks and bonds. All the real estate was mortgaged. So what's left is a measly 150 grand? That does not make for gracious living. Nancy sloshed the wine in her glass. They would go through that in six months.

But . . . there is one other asset: life insurance. On Bud.

The one smart thing she did right after their son was born, and back when the Jarvisons were the wealthiest family in northern Wisconsin, was take out a $20 million life insurance policy on Bud. The trust manager assured her those premiums had been paid faithfully over the years so that was one piece of good news.

All she needed now was for Bud to drop dead. *I wish*, thought Nancy. In spite of his heavy drinking and bad diet, Bud was remarkably healthy. Given his genetic history, he would likely live well into his eighties.

A clatter of fireworks in the distance caught her attention: damn picnickers down at the public beach. For some reason, tourists in the Northwoods felt compelled to celebrate the Fourth through the entire *month* of July. She had complained numerous times with no results. The word "tourist" spelled money and no one, not even the local police, were eager to ruin a tourist's holiday.

But the sound of bursting fireworks gave her an idea.

Chapter Thirty-Four

It was 7:30 when Bud finally got home, his heavy figure slouching into the family room where Nancy sat curled up on the sofa watching television and reading magazines. His shoulders drooped. Circles of sweat had dried around the armpits of his golf shirt. And the man who prided himself on shaving twice a day looked grungy in his five o'clock shadow. He was not drunk.

"Sorry to be so late," he said, dropping his body with a thud onto the ottoman in front of his easy chair.

"Oh, I'm sure you have a good excuse," said Nancy, chewing gum while flipping the pages of the *Town & Country* magazine she held in her hands.

Bud lifted his head and gave her a long look, the expression in his eyes so dark she felt a frisson of fear. It was a look she hadn't seen since the day he had to tell her their son was dead.

"It has not been a good day." He dropped his gaze, studying the floor as he talked. "I was on the seventh hole at the club when a couple Federal agents walked up. They arrested me."

Nancy looked up from her magazine, startled. "I'm sorry. Did you say *arrested*?"

"Jeff was in my foursome," he said, referring to their family lawyer and his good friend from college days. "He got me out on bail. They're picking me up in the morning and taking me to Federal Court in Green Bay."

Nancy was quiet. She swung her legs off the sofa and sat up straight. She spat out her gum, tore off a corner of the magazine cover, and wrapped her gum in it. "I don't understand."

"It's blackmail. I made one mistake, just one *little* mistake." Bud looked at his wife, shaking his finger.

"What do you mean 'blackmail'?" asked Nancy. "The police are—"

"Not the police—it's the FBI and the DEA. They're accusing me of money laundering and drug trafficking."

A long silence hung in the room.

"Bud, does this have anything to do with that drug bust I heard about on the Channel 12 news tonight?"

"I was just trying to help some migrant workers start a business." He looked down at the floor again.

"You? Start a business? What—a pot-farming business?" Nancy's voice grew shrill.

"I didn't know," he threw up a hand. "You know I'm no gardener."

"And I'm no idiot. Did you know what you were doing when you impregnated that girl?"

"How do you know about that?" Bud's head snapped up. "She's a sweet kid. Miguel's sister and—"

"No details, please. Talk to Jeff and arrange the usual settlement."

"Wish I could. Too late."

"Bud, just tell me how you got roped into this?"

"It started with the girl, Angel. I got together with her a couple times at the Thunder Bay Bar. Next thing I knew her brother—that's Miguel—heard I owned banks and told me he would tell you about the pregnancy if I didn't help him out. I felt so bad after I lost all that money, I couldn't stand the thought of him telling you that, too. So I agreed to deposit cash for him that he could wire down to his people in Mexico. That's all I did—I just deposited the money. I thought it would be just the one time but he kept insisting."

Nancy stared at Bud. Something didn't fit. He'd been guilty of indiscretions before and been chagrined when she found out—but then he would breeze on to the next one. Truth was people always fixed things for Bud, whether it was a lawyer, a friend—even herself. For one simple reason: it had always been worth it. Now that she thought about it, over the past few months Bud had been spending as if he still had millions. He had rented a huge yacht on Lake Superior for two weeks that cost $20,000, and he had treated five buddies to a week of walleye fishing in Canada at one of the fancy lodges up there—another big chunk of change.

"Tell me, what *exactly* did you get out of this arrangement besides keeping your little secret?"

"Twenty percent. That's how come I didn't have to drain the trust to pay our taxes and I bought you that diamond tennis bracelet. I mean, Nancy, I'm down to our last hundred grand. We're broke. I had to do something."

"I see. So what happens next? You go to prison?"

"It's all about what happened earlier today. Miguel is cooperating with the Feds. He's hoping to get asylum or in the witness protection program so he's telling them everything. And, yeah, I guess I'm going to prison."

"For money laundering."

"And drug trafficking and murder."

"*Murder?*"

"Excuse me, Mrs. Jarvison?" Cynthia poked her head through the door from the kitchen. "Do you need anything more before I—"

"Oh, for chrissake!" Nancy threw up her hands in exasperation. "How stupid are you? Don't you know when people are having a private conversation? No—I don't need a goddamn thing. Now leave us alone."

"Sorry," said Cynthia, ducking as she pulled the door closed.

"A couple people were killed when they got too close to where Miguel's people were growing things and were shot. I'm considered an accomplice. Like I said, it's been a bad day." Bud heaved a sigh.

"So you go to prison, I pay your legal bills, and what else?"

"I have to pay a fine. But it *is* tax deductible."

"Well, isn't *that* a glimmer of good news," said Nancy, dripping sarcasm. "How big a fine?"

"Not sure. I'll know later—maybe tomorrow."

"Bud, give me a hint. When this is all over will we have *anything* left?"

He didn't answer and he didn't look up. "If you don't mind, I'm going to take a shower, then go down to have one last drink in the boat—or maybe six. Might be the last night I get to enjoy it."

"Have six, Bud," said Nancy, relaxing back on the sofa. "You deserve it. You *have* had a very bad day." She gave a soft chuckle. "What the hell—at this point all we can do is laugh, right?"

"I guess so," said Bud with a rueful chuckle of his own. Before he left the room, he paused to kiss her on the forehead.

Watching him leave, Nancy realized that was the first time in years that they had laughed together. Years.

She waited until she heard the shower running, then she ran outside, across the lawn, and down the stairs to the dock. Moving fast, she checked the boat storage areas to be sure Bud hadn't stashed a gun somewhere. With the exception of three bottles of Jack Daniels and glassware in dire need of a good washing, she found nothing. Satisfied, she ran back up to the house. The last thing she needed was for him to commit suicide.

Chapter Thirty-Five

It was 1:30 in the morning when she peered through the kitchen window and down across the sloping lawn. The boat was dark. Clouds obscured the moon, turning the lake black. A light breeze in the warm air sent ripples toward shore. Nancy hoped it wouldn't rain: This was one night when she needed tourists enjoying a boozy late night on the beach. Her .357 Magnum Smith & Wesson was loaded and ready, its walnut box with the velvet lining open on the kitchen table.

She had owned the gun since she was seventeen and inherited it from her grandfather. When she was a girl of eleven, he had taught her how to shoot a .22 pistol, arguing that she needed to be able to defend herself against the overly attentive, be it men or mother bears. He had felt it important that a woman be able to do two things: ride a horse and shoot a gun. He was pleased when she proved she could do both.

When he died, she had asked her father for her grandfather's .357 Smith & Wesson. It was a beautiful gun with a handsome wood grip. And it held six rounds. More than what she might need. Tonight the hard part would be steadying the gun: Her left shoulder was still sore.

She crept down the stairs and onto the dock, hoping the wooden planks wouldn't give her away. She needn't have worried. The loud snoring from the interior of the boat covered any noise she might make.

Cautiously, she slipped down the ladder into the boat. Bud was asleep on the padded bench behind the table where he and his buddies played poker. He lay on his back, his head on a canvas pillow, mouth open, snoring loudly. One of her Baccarat cocktail tumblers had fallen onto the carpet under his dangling left hand, leaving a wet stain.

Aiming at his forehead, Nancy fired once. The years of anger surged as she stood there and she fired again. And again. Once more. Fireworks always went off four or more times. She climbed back out of the boat and started up the stairs toward the deck off the kitchen. Just as she turned to look back at the boat, the moon escaped from the clouds. A curtain in the boathouse apartment moved.

She had forgotten Cynthia was sleeping there. Nancy shrugged. Probably just the wind. If not, Cynthia could be persuaded she'd heard fireworks. Meantime, the house phone, an eighties-style landline she kept in the kitchen, was ringing.

"Mrs. Jarvison," said a voice gravelly with sleep. "Doug Stafford two docks down from you. Did you hear all that noise? Sounded more like gunshots than fireworks and awfully close to your place. Should we call someone?'

"You know, I think it was some idiot down on the public beach with bottle rockets but I called the cops, Doug. They're checking it out. And thank you for your concern. I appreciate it."

Setting the cordless phone back on its stand, she considered her next move. No doubt she would have been wise to throw the gun out into the lake—that's what criminals always did on TV. On the other hand, the lake was so shallow near their dock that the gun could be found easily. *Found is putting it mildly*, thought Nancy. Their lake was so crystal clear that you can stand on the dock and see everything on the bottom a good twenty feet out and then some. No, she would be better off getting rid of it somewhere else. And then only if she really had to: after all, it had belonged to her grandfather, the only man who had never betrayed her. A rush of sadness caught her off guard. Thank goodness her grandfather was dead. He would have been so disappointed to know who she had become.

She set the gun back in its box, tucked the velvet lining over it and, opening the long drawer where she kept the laundered bed linens, she shoved the box under and back. It left a barely discernible bump. She found some folded pillowcases and set them over it to reinforce a reason for the slight bulge in the linens.

Before going up to bed, Nancy checked to be sure Cynthia had set the timer for the coffee. What time was Bud expecting to be picked up? Six or seven? She couldn't remember so she changed the timer to six A.M.

Chapter Thirty-Six

The white impatiens lining the Jarvisons' circle drive glistened with dew under the morning sun as a black SUV drove up on the dot of seven the next morning. Watching from the living room, coffee mug in hand, Nancy turned away for a moment to check her image in the hall mirror.

She had slept so well it had been a struggle to look sleep-deprived but she thought she was managing: no makeup, hair tossed to one side to appear limp. To herself, at least, she looked bad. A hesitant, faltering voice should complete the impression.

"Good morning, gentlemen," she said, opening the front door. "My husband is still sleeping. He was up most of the night . . . actually we both were. He told me you were coming at eight—" She dropped her eyes as if in pain.

"We're sorry, Mrs. Jarvison," said the first man. He was dressed in a dark suit that fit so badly she figured he must buy his clothes at Walmart. "I'm Alan Strickland with the FBI and my colleague here is Ron Hardin with the DEA, I mean, ah, the Drug Enforcement—"

"I know what DEA stands for," said Nancy in a blunt tone. Treating her like she was an idiot was so annoying she forgot about keeping her voice small.

"Well, good," said the man named Alan. He hesitated before saying, "I, ah, is your husband available?"

Ignoring his request, Nancy blocked the way into the hall saying, "I don't believe a word those drug dealing monsters have said. How can you believe criminals? My husband is a good man. He has done so much for our community—"

"The details will be straightened out, Mrs. Jarvison," said Alan Strickland, looking fatigued himself. "If he is innocent, he'll be fine. This morning is a formality and very likely we'll have him back home late this afternoon. Please. Tell him we're here."

Nancy gave the two men a grim look then called up the hall stairway, "Bud, honey, they're here. Are you ready, sweetheart?" She waited for an answer. "He may be in the shower. I'll go check." She ran up the stairs, walked through the master bedroom, adjusted the coverlet and pillows and lingered another minute before walking back to the top of the stairs.

"I don't see him. But he likes to have his morning coffee down on the dock or on the deck of his boat. Oh, now I remember. I'm so sorry. He got up in the middle of the night. He may have fallen asleep down there. I didn't fall asleep until four maybe and then just woke up myself so—"

"That's all right, Mrs. Jarvison. We'll check the boat."

"Are you sure? I'm happy to—but okay."

"Is this the door to the kitchen?" Strickland asked as Nancy came down the stairs.

"Yes," she said, pointing. "If you'll go through there, you'll see the sliding doors that open to the deck and the walkway down toward the dock."

The two men walked through the kitchen. They slid open the door to the deck and ran across the lawn toward the boathouse and the luxurious yacht moored there.

Nancy watched from the kitchen window. When she saw the two men emerge from the boat, she couldn't help but smile to herself. She tried to look busy at the small antique desk where she kept her calendar and household lists. She looked up as Alan rushed in.

"What? What's wrong?" She kept her voice noncommittal. "If he's not there, he may be in his workshop. That's the building behind the garage. He does woodworking to relax. Better than Prozac, you know." She managed to produce an ingratiating and pained smile.

"When was the last time you saw your husband?"

"Well . . . um . . . right around midnight. Bud has sleep apnea so we don't share a bedroom—we haven't in years. He wears one of those noisy machines that keep his heart from stopping or something like that. Yes, it was late last night." She dropped her voice conspiratorially. "He was drinking pretty heavily and I couldn't . . . well, I don't blame him. The man is devastated. Why?"

"Your husband is dead. He's been shot."

"Oh no." Nancy slumped in her chair. "I was afraid he might do that. I thought I made sure all his guns were locked in the gun cabinet up in his study. He must have hid one from me. This is all my fault—poor Bud." She dropped her face into her hands.

"He did not commit suicide. Someone killed your husband, Mrs. Jarvison."

She popped her head up to stare at Strickland, a stunned look on her face. "That's preposterous. You're trying to trick me."

The two men stared at her, saying nothing. Nancy looked from one face to the other.

"You're sure? You're sure he's not just . . . if that's true, you people are responsible." She shook an angry finger at them. "You should have been protecting him—protecting *us*." She raised her voice to a near scream. "It's your fault those drug people came after Bud."

Alan raised his hands, gesturing for her to quiet down.

While the DEA agent walked off to the far corner of the kitchen to make a call, Alan Strickland pulled up a kitchen chair to sit beside Nancy. "How much do you know about your husband's involvement with the drug operation?"

"Nothing. Not one iota. All he ever told me he was helping a young immigrant family start a farming business—potatoes and blueberries. The money he deposited for them was their first harvest of berries." Nancy's voice faltered. "He said he had set up a foundation that would bring more families into that business."

Through tears she tried to speak clearly. "Bud told me he thought he was being a mentor to that young man. He had no idea they were growing *marijuana*. Bud and I don't even know what that looks like." She inhaled, pressing tissues to her eyes as she ground out her words.

The back door opened and Cynthia walked into the kitchen. She stopped at the sight of the two men and Nancy. "Mrs. Jarvison, what's wrong?"

"This is my housekeeper," said Nancy in a hoarse voice. "She stays in the apartment above the boathouse. Maybe she saw them. Maybe she heard them."

"Heard who? What?" asked Cynthia, her eyes widening. "I heard loud fireworks sometime after midnight—woke me up they were so loud. If that's what you mean. But that happens all the time when people are partying late at the public beach. I'm kinda used to it or I'd never get any sleep."

"We just found Mr. Jarvison dead in his boat. He's been shot," said Alan.

Nancy peered at Cynthia through her tissues. The look of shock on Cynthia's face was so genuine that Nancy felt relief. She must not have seen a thing last night.

Chapter Thirty-Seven

Osborne was on his third cup of coffee at Ray's when his cell phone rang.

"Hi, Dad, where are you?" asked Erin, sounding cheerful for the first time in days. "Can you call Ray for me? Cody is doing so well that the hospital is releasing him today. Ray has called at least three times insisting he help us pack up. But he might be out fishing with a client."

"No, hon, he just got back. He's right here—we're having coffee together. How soon are you leaving the hospital?"

"In an hour."

"We'll be there in a few minutes." Osborne clicked off his phone and got to his feet. "Ready for action?"

"You bet," said Ray, reaching for the shopping bag he had set aside for their mission. "If we get arrested, I'll take the fall, old man."

When they got to the hospital, they went straight to Cody's room. Erin had an overnight case in which she had brought Cody fresh clothing to wear home. All the gifts, including the hat with the stuffed trout, were stacked on the bed. Cody sat in a nearby chair, a baleful look on his face. The good news was he was sitting up; the bad news was how sad he looked.

"I can't take anything home except my clothes, Grandpa," he said. He looked up at Ray, tears glistening in his eyes, and said, "not even my magic fish hat."

"Not to worry, kiddo," said Ray. He reached for the hat and stuffed it into the shopping bag.

"Wait, this too," said Osborne, grabbing *Lunkers Love Nightcrawlers* and shoving the book into the bag with the hat.

"Stop it, you two," said Erin. "The hospital instructions are quite clear: *no items are allowed to leave the isolation ward.* They may be contaminated. Even Cody's clothes that he was wearing when he was admitted have to be discarded. That's the rule, guys."

"And you're going to follow that stupid rule?" asked Ray.

"Yes, I am going to follow the stupid rule. Now put everything back. Please. Dad? You, too. Put that book back where it was."

Just then, Cody's doctor walked into the room. "Hi, fella, just came to say goodbye and thank you for being such a good patient. Hey, what's wrong?"

Cody burst into tears. "They won't let me have my magic fish hat."

"What hat are you talking about?" asked the doctor, looking confused.

"This hat," said Ray, pulling the hat out of the shopping bag. "I had it made special for Cody."

"Yes," said Osborne, "and we have a special book too."

Cody sobbed, "My nightcrawler book." He resumed an energetic bawling.

"Can we all settle down?" asked the doctor. "This is not a problem. Yes, we have a general policy for patients in isolation but I can waive it. The fact is the type of meningitis that Cody had is caused by a bacterium that survives only a minute or two outside the body. It cannot live on things like that hat or the book." He turned to Erin. "If it makes you feel better, you can put both in the freezer for half an hour but, trust me, all these gifts including the hat and the book are safe to take home."

"So I don't . . . *have* . . . to steal the items?" asked Ray.

"Absolutely not. I'll walk out with you folks just to be sure you don't have a problem. Now, Cody, wipe those tears, okay, son?"

Cody sniffed and smiled and stood up. To see that child walking filled Osborne's heart. The day was looking good.

Chapter Thirty-Eight

"This time of year I like . . ." Ray paused as he cast toward the sky ". . . to fish muskie from late afternoon . . . to midnight." Standing beside him on the pontoon, Jake watched Ray reel in his lure, finishing with his arms extended to make a wide figure eight swirl at the side of the boat.

"And when I fish later like this . . ." again the lure flew from Ray's spinning rod ". . . I prefer bucktails with larger blades . . . those big girls can sense the vibrations through the dark, doncha know." Ray grinned. "And that's what you got on there, Jake."

"Big girls?" asked Jake. "Why do you call them that?"

"With muskies, it's the female fish who grow larger, fight harder . . . it's like life . . . isn't it always about the women?"

"Well, okay then," said Jake, smiling. "I'm not going to argue that one."

"Nothing makes Ray happier than night fishing," said Lew. She stood near Osborne at the rear of the big pontoon. The evening breezes were calm enough that she and Osborne could cast without fear of snagging one another.

"What are you using, Lew?" asked Jake. "A bucktail like Ray's?"

"Oh no, tonight I'm trying out a six-inch slammer in the Red Dragon color. It's got a nice tight wobble to it. Last summer a friend of mine caught fifty muskies using a Red Dragon. Doc here is fishing his favorite: a yellow mud puppy surface bait. We'll see who wins—or none of us may. This is a tough time of year to catch muskies, Jake. When the water warms up, the big ones suspend over deep water. You might want to ask Ray if you should add a half-ounce weight to that bait of yours to get it deeper."

"Will I know when I get a strike?" asked Jake. "Or is it like tenkara that I need to see or feel a change in the drift?"

"Oh, you'll know," said Lew as she cast the slammer. "If a big girl hits, you'll think you caught the bottom of the lake. And muskies are unpredictable. They can come toward your bait from the right or the left or drop down so sudden it's like they came right out of the sky. Or they can come so hard they'll knock you down."

"Lew's right about that," said Osborne. "They can catch you off balance and wham! I learned a long time ago to use Garcia Ambassadeur reels for just that reason. That reel is built so that once a muskie hits the fish can't snap the handle out of your hand, which happens with too many other reels."

"Now . . . the key to *landing* a muskie," said Ray, "is once you think you've got a follow, bring your lure toward the boat . . . but keep it in the water doing the figure eight move . . . like this."

Jake leaned over to watch Ray's rod as he swirled the lure close to the side of the pontoon.

As dusk fell, Osborne let his thoughts wander while he listened to the soft patter of his friends' voices, their words as smooth as ripples on the water. He relished the serenity of an evening like this: the lake holding bands of ivory and silver crisscrossed with streams of diamonds cast by the setting sun. And he had an invitation to Lew's place later. The promise of her warm roughness calmed his heart.

"Awfully nice of you folks to take me out this evening," said Jake. "I've never tried muskie fishing."

"Fair trade," said Lew. "Doc and I had never even heard of tenkara fly-fishing much less had an opportunity to learn how to do it. I love it—takes me out of myself if that makes sense. Maybe we can do it again before you leave?"

"We'll have to save it for my next visit. I'm heading home tomorrow. Your colleague from the crime lab, Bruce, was kind enough to deliver my son's remains to the funeral home for cremation. I've been told I can pick up his ashes early in the morning."

"I hope it helps a little to know what happened," said Lew, "that he was shot by one of the drug traffickers guarding the marijuana operation."

"Does anything help when you lose the person you love most?" asked Jake. "Losing Liam will never be easy for me but Bruce told me he was sure my son never knew he'd been shot. His last thought had to be one of getting ready to cast his tenkara fly rod."

"I'll vouch for that," said Ray. "Those guys had Winchester Model 70 rifles . . . 30-06 caliber with telescopic sights on 'em. Classic sniper rifles . . . Sheriff Moore told me."

The pontoon drifted on, the only sound the whir of a lure flying out and over nearby weed beds.

"What's the latest on that drug crew anyway?" asked Ray, setting his muskie rod down as he reached into the cooler. "Coke? Ginger ale . . . anyone? Jake, Chief . . . either of you want a beer . . . I got a couple Spotted Cow brewskis."

"I'll have a Spotted Cow," said Jake.

"Ginger ales for myself and Doc," said Lew. "Thanks, Ray."

"Alan got himself an unbelievable break," said Lew. "The guy running the operation, Miguel Estevez is his name, is cooperating 100 percent. He's hoping to avoid getting deported and is bargaining to get into the Witness Protection Program, which may be impossible since he isn't a U.S. citizen.

"On the other hand, given the valuable information he's been providing to the FBI and the DEA, I expect they'll go easy on him. By the way, that woman who is pregnant is Miguel's wife and they really want to stay in the country if they can, even if Miguel does prison time."

"So Bud was not the father of her child?" said Ray.

"No. But Bud didn't know that," said Lew. "Turns out she was bait. Miguel met Bud at the casino one night when Bud was losing at craps and the casino cut off his credit. Miguel had been watching and offered to loan him $1,000. This was right on the heels of Bud's losses in the stock market and he was drinking heavily. Didn't take long for Miguel to learn his new friend was a not-so-smart drunk who was well connected to banks and chased women: an easy mark.

"Not long after loaning Bud the thousand bucks, Miguel asked for a small favor in return: He wanted Bud to handle cash deposits for him. The money would go into the Jarvison branch in Loon Lake and be transferred to a financial institution in Chicago that had a subsidiary in Mexico City. A simple transaction.

"Miguel offered Bud 20 percent of each bundle of cash. With three to five deposits a week averaging just under ten grand, the FBI thinks Bud was clearing as much as forty grand a month since last September. Good money for a guy who just lost his shirt in the stock market.

"That's when poor Peter Corbin made his big mistake. He flagged the sequence of the deposits, not realizing Bud was behind them. Then feeling he owed it to the chairman of the bank's parent company, he alerted Bud that he would be filing a Suspicious Activity Report on behalf of the bank. He thought he was doing a good thing. He thought that would earn him a bonus if not a promotion.

"At that point we think Bud responded in a very friendly way. He asked him to hold off until Bud could notify his other bank executives and in the meantime invited Corbin to a weekend of snowmobiling up at his hunting lodge—an executive perk. Bud lured him out onto the Pine River after alerting Miguel to have one of his guards prepared to shoot Corbin as they drove their sleds along the river. Bruce told me the other day that the crime lab confirmed that the patterns of blunt trauma to Corbin's skull and the shattered section of the snowmobile helmet match. Peter Corbin did not drown, he was shot."

"You keep that crime lab busy, don't you?" said Jake with a smile.

"This week I have," said Lew. "Most of those Wausau boys can be hard to work with but Bruce is terrific. He's smart, he knows his science, and he is transparent. With Bruce I know what I'm getting. I feel sorry for him right now—all this beautiful weather, great for night fishing, and that poor guy is over digging bullets out of Bud Jarvison's boat."

"Do they know who shot Bud?" asked Osborne as he changed his lure from a mudpuppy to a Pikie Minnow. "Someone from the cartel?"

"That's what Alan and the DEA guy think. What puzzles me is how did the cartel know so soon?"

"Doc, you and Ray were there that night. You know we surprised the hell out of Miguel and the whole crew. They were so panicked by the wolf howls, everyone except Miguel forgot their phones—and we grabbed Miguel's right away. Alan checked that phone and no calls or texts had been made within an hour of the arrests."

"Consider the reverse," said Jake. "What if *not* hearing from Miguel was a signal?"

"Good point," said Lew, "especially since Alan arrested Bud early Monday on the golf course and we had Miguel under interrogation all that day, too. I'll check on that. Monday may have been a day when the connections in Mexico expected deposits to be wired south—so when nothing came through, they became suspicious. They sure acted fast, though. Bud was killed less than twenty-four hours after his arrest."

"Someone flew in from Chicago is my bet," said Ray.

"Right now they're looking to find out who in the Chicago financial institution was responsible for wiring the money to

Mexico," said Lew, "but that's Alan's headache. My concern is who killed Bud Jarvison and very likely we'll end up with a victim murdered by 'parties unknown.' Murdered by parties unknown and bamboozled into thinking he was going to be a father. According to Alan that was the one time during the interrogation Monday that Bud brightened up—when he admitted to an affair with Angel."

"But what was that all about . . . if the woman is Miguel's wife?" asked Ray. "How could Bud not know that?"

"Consider the drinking," said Lew. "Bud was never 100 percent alert when he was at the casino. According to Miguel, he had a habit of being three sheets to the wind by the time Miguel and Angel arrived. She would entice him to a room at the casino hotel where she would spike his drink and he'd pass out. When he came to, she would say they had been intimate. Bud, of course, couldn't remember and not remembering was nothing new to him. Plus Angel and Miguel managed to produce some incriminating photos taken while Bud was passed out."

"So Angel was Miguel's insurance . . . in case Bud ever balked at making the deposits?" asked Ray.

"If Bud hadn't lost his fortune, I think he could have weathered the paternity issue but he was so close to bankruptcy he was desperate. He could not afford the kind of financial settlement he had made in the past with women, which is why he was reluctant to have Nancy learn about Angel's pregnancy. That would involve paternity and paternity means money."

"And as we know," said Osborne, "Nancy is all about the money. Always has been."

Chapter Thirty-Nine

Two nights later, after deciding the sunset was too fine to miss, Osborne and Lew rushed down the stone stairs to his dock. They made it in time—the sky was magnificent with billows of orange and a pale peach shot with streaks of fire. The warm air was a caress on the skin, the lake still.

As they settled into the cushions on the chaise lounges that Osborne kept on the dock in hopes of nights like this Lew said, "I had an interesting phone call today. I didn't want to bring it up in the middle of dinner with Erin's family and ruin our celebration of your grandson's return to the living."

"'Return to the living' puts it mildly," said Osborne. "I don't remember the kid ever having that much energy." He smiled at the memory of Cody jumping up and down while pumping both arms when Osborne had announced they would be fishing with Ray that Saturday.

Aware that sound would carry easily over the water, Lew kept her voice low as she said, "An insurance executive called me today with a question about Bud Jarvison's death. Seems there was a $20 million life insurance policy on Bud and his widow would like it to be paid in one lump sum."

"A recent policy?" Osborne looked at Lew. "That would be interesting."

"No. It was taken out years ago when Bud was in his early thirties. His father was still alive and the premiums have been paid annually out of the family trust. Nothing suspicious."

"That means the policy would have been taken out before their son was killed—when the family still had all their wealth. So what was his question?"

"Was I sure that Bud's death wasn't a suicide."

"Your answer?"

"You can shoot yourself in the head once with a .357 Smith & Wesson but not four times."

"Was he convinced?"

"I believe so. He's a hunter himself so he knew what I was saying."

The sound of someone knocking on a door followed by footsteps along the side of the house caused Osborne to sit up to look in the direction of the noise. At the same time, the dog ran toward the stairs, barking loudly.

"Dr. Osborne," called a woman's voice. "It's me, Cynthia Baron."

"Cynthia? Is something wrong?" Peering up, Osborne could barely make out the woman's figure standing in the shadows. He hurried up the stairs.

"I'm so sorry, I know it's late," she said as Osborne came around the corner of the house. He pulled open the screen door. "It's okay. Come in, please. Have a seat at the kitchen table. Something to drink? Water? A soda?"

Walking ahead of him, Cynthia pulled out a kitchen chair, sat down, and cupped her right hand over her eyes as if pushing back tears.

"Cynthia, is someone hurt? One of your children?"

"No, no, no," she said as she shook her head. She looked up with sad eyes and said, "I am so worried, Dr. Osborne. I have made a terrible mistake." Cynthia grasped both hands tight in her lap, her shoulders shaking.

"Try to calm down and tell me about it."

"You must think it's strange that I'm coming to you for advice but you know me and my family and you've helped me before. Last week, when I was working at the Jarvisons', I heard you say that you help the police, that you're a deputy."

"Dental forensics, Cynthia. I help them identify victims through dental records. That's all. No more than that. I am not a police officer."

"Can I help?" asked Lew. She had entered the house so quietly that Osborne hadn't heard her approaching.

Cynthia paled. She threw a look of anguish at Osborne. Glancing crazily from one to the other, Cynthia blurted, "I'm guilty of withholding information. I couldn't help it. I needed the money. I had to." She was sobbing before she could finish.

"Doc, would you please run a little cold water on that paper towel by the sink and hand it to me?" asked Lew in a calm voice.

Osborne did as he was told. Lew took the cold compress and held it against Cynthia's forehead and eyes.

"Kleenex, please." After a couple deep breaths, Cynthia blew her nose. "Okay, let's start from the beginning," said Lew.

"Um, in the middle of the night last Monday, I was asleep in the boathouse at the Jarvisons' when I heard these explosions. Couldn't be sure if I heard gunshots or fireworks. I just lay still for a few minutes. When I didn't hear any more, I peeked through the curtains. I could see Mrs. Jarvison up on the deck outside the kitchen. It was dark but when the moon lit up the yard for a moment, I thought I saw a gun in her hand. She was holding something, I know."

"But let's be specific. You're saying you *thought* you saw Nancy Jarvison holding a gun?" asked Lew.

"I wasn't sure. She was standing still and then I heard the kitchen phone ringing so I assumed she might have called the cops about the fireworks—she did that a lot."

"Did you go up to the house?"

Cynthia sighed. "No. When nothing more happened, I told myself maybe all I heard were fireworks and maybe she wasn't holding a gun. I, um, went back to bed. The next day after they found Mr. Jarvison and the police had gone Mrs. Jarvison started acting really weird. That night she made me help her take his bedroom and study apart. She dumped all his clothes in my car and told me to give everything away.

"Then she took garbage bags and threw everything that was his in the trash—pictures, belts, and cufflinks, all his wood carvings and duck decoys that he kept in his den—everything except his guns. Those she had me take to that auction house in Rhinelander and sell them for whatever they would pay. She didn't care how much either. She told me she wanted everything of Mr. Jarvison's gone or destroyed."

"All his fishing gear?" asked Osborne. "Like reels and lures and—"

"Everything. I saved this little wooden box though. The one you asked me about. She had thrown that into the garbage bags with everything else."

Cynthia pulled the wooden box from a pocket in her jacket and handed it to Osborne. He turned it over: a red seal marked the bottom. Osborne opened it. Liam's two trout flies were still there.

"This is Liam Barber's wooden fly box. His father will be so happy to get this, Cynthia. Thank you. Did Bud ever mention where he found it?"

"After you asked about it, when I was dusting in the den, I asked about it. He said he was walking his property line by some land he owned along the Wisconsin River and found it lying on the river bank."

Lew snorted. "Property line, my eye. He was walking the shoreline of the Pine River with his business partner, Miguel, checking out the pot plantation."

"Back up, Cynthia," said Osborne. "Would you say that you aren't *sure* if you saw a gun in Nancy Jarvison's hand that night?"

"Yes. It crossed my mind at the time but I didn't think about it seriously until Mr. Jarvison was found dead. I mean, as dark as it was, she could have been holding a big flashlight or something."

"Fine," said Lew. "Let's leave it at this for the moment. If we find other evidence that indicates she may have had a gun, then we can revisit your impression. Meanwhile, you have given me this information with a legitimate caveat that you may be wrong. Cynthia, there's an old saying in law enforcement that the worst witness is an eyewitness." Lew smiled and patted Cynthia's hand. "Meantime, thank you for being brave enough to come forward."

"There's more." Cynthia's voice steadied.

"More?"

"Yes. One of my duties at the Jarvisons' is to iron all the sheets and pillowcases. Mrs. Jarvison is a perfectionist and she likes to have their beds changed every day. After the sheets are ironed, they are folded and kept in drawers in the linen closet on the first floor. Once a week I wash and iron the duvet covers for the down comforters.

"I'm always careful to put the linens away just so—in case she checks to see if I'm doing it right. I did it wrong once and she docked me $50 on my pay that week.

"So the Saturday before Mr. Jarvison was shot, I finished the ironing and put the sheets away as always. But Monday morning when I went to check for a fresh duvet cover for her bed, I saw one bunched at the back of the drawer where the covers are kept. And some pillowcases were there that I usually keep in a different drawer—so I was worried I'd made a mistake. I moved those but the lump was still there so thinking that one of the covers had gotten shoved back there by accident, I pulled the drawer out to check. See, if you didn't open that drawer as often as I do, you would not notice the slight bump. The bump wasn't a duvet cover—it was a box."

Cynthia held her hands out to indicate the box was just over a foot in length. "It's a box with a gun inside. A handgun of some kind. And it looks expensive."

"Is it there now?" asked Lew.

"Yes, I checked tonight while she was out with friends. The reason I didn't tell you earlier is because today was my last day. The Jarvisons owed me $1,500 and she wouldn't pay me until today. I was afraid if I told you anything and she got arrested that I would never be paid." Cynthia faltered. "I'm sorry. The money I made there this summer, it's all I have."

Lew wasn't listening—she was on her cell phone calling the dispatch center. "Marlaine? Is Todd Donovan on duty tonight? Good, I thought so. Would you reach him and ask him to stand by. I'm going to need his help with a search warrant in, oh, about an hour or so. Thanks."

Lew punched more numbers on the phone and reached the county judge. Osborne heard her say she would be stopping by his home with a search warrant to be signed. He must have asked an obvious question because she said, "Can it wait? For a murder weapon? I don't think that's wise. Thanks, Judge, I'll be by within half an hour."

"You're going to the Jarvisons' tonight?" asked Cynthia.

"Oh yes," said Lew. "We don't want to give anyone time to move that gun."

"Let me show you right where to look," said Cynthia. "Dr. Osborne, do you have a piece of paper?"

Chapter Forty

It was after midnight when Lew and Osborne drove up the long drive to the Jarvison house. As if auditioning for Christmas, precisely planted and trimmed balsams were spaced along the winding road, which ended in the circle drive fronting the house. The house was dark.

Before getting out of the car, Lew checked the map that Cynthia had drawn. It indicated that the linen closet was located at the back of the house. It could be reached through a narrow hall to the left of the kitchen. The foyer and front hall of the house led straight back to the kitchen.

Lew had asked Osborne to accompany her saying, "You know Nancy Jarvison. Having you there may encourage her to be courteous, which—"

"No need to explain," said Osborne. "I've known the woman for years. I'll take the bullet—just kidding."

They both knew he wasn't kidding. They expected nastiness and using Osborne as a target might make it easier for Lew to conduct the search.

A second squad car pulled up behind them. With the flash of his headlights in her rearview mirror, Lew opened the car door.

"Good. We've got backup. I told Todd to watch the back of the house, too, just in case. Let's go in, Doc."

Lew rang the front door bell. No response. She rang again . . . and again. "Okay," she said, "I'll try the door but let me alert Todd in case a security system goes off."

No sooner had she spoken than the heavy front door swung open. A disheveled Nancy Jarvison holding a white cotton robe tight against her chest stood blinking in the glare from the police car headlights.

"What on earth do you want at this hour?" She may have been asleep but the slurring of her words indicated more than a little self-medication.

"I have a search warrant, Mrs. Jarvison," said Lew, holding out the document as she spoke, "for a specific location in your home. Won't take me more than five or ten minutes."

"Oh for chrissake come back in the goddamn morning." Nancy moved to slam the front door but Lew stuck out one foot and the door bounced back.

"Here, Mrs. Jarvison, please read this so you know—" Before Lew could finish her sentence Nancy grabbed the warrant from her, blinked at the page, and shoved it back at her. "Go right ahead."

It was obvious to Osborne she had no idea where Lew was headed. Nor did she seem concerned when Lew walked straight down the front hall and through the doorway to the kitchen. Still clutching her robe, Nancy weaved her way down the hall behind Osborne who was following Lew. Osborne began to suspect she wasn't as drunk as she seemed: Her eyes were watchful.

Lew walked through the kitchen and turned left to go down the hallway toward the linen closet. Halfway down the hall, Nancy grabbed Osborne by the arm.

"Stop," said Nancy. "Why do you want the utility room? Nothing down there—that's the laundry. I mean all that's there is my goddamn washer and dryer."

Lew didn't answer. She was standing in front of the doors lining the left side of the wall and leaning over to open the large middle drawer when Nancy pushed Osborne out of the way.

"Stop!" Head down, Nancy ran at Lew.

Head butt or tackle, Osborne didn't wait to find out. Before she reached Lew, he grabbed Nancy by the waist and yanked her to her knees. Todd appeared behind them. The young officer pushed past Osborne to kneel on Nancy's back as he forced her arms back and slipped handcuffs onto her wrists.

Nancy lay quiet as Lew pulled open the drawer. In the drawer were the neatly folded duvet covers, one on top of the other, just as Cynthia had described. Lew pulled the drawer out farther until she could see the slight bulge in the back. Reaching under the covers, she felt the outline of something long, flat, and hard. Stepping over Nancy, who remained face down on the floor, Lew walked back into the kitchen and set the wooden case on the kitchen table.

She reached for the Nitrile gloves that she had slipped into her pocket earlier and pulled them on. She opened the case. A .357 Smith & Wesson with a wood grip lay on the velvet cloth lining the box. Only two of the six rounds it had held remained.

She looked up at Osborne and said, "I wonder how Nancy looks in orange."

Chapter Forty-One

"You know, Doc, if Nancy Jarvison had not insisted on having her sheets ironed, she might have gotten away with murder," said Lew, leaning back against the captain's chair on Ray's pontoon. Legs braced on the railing with her ankles crossed, she closed her eyes and let the morning sun play across her face. It was a perfect July morning—late morning that is.

"Is the ballistics report in from Bruce yet?" asked Osborne.

He was on his knees searching through his tackle box for the sinkers and hooks he wanted. He had been disappointed earlier when he stopped by two different bait shops hoping to buy nightcrawlers only to find they were sold out. The first shop, his favorite and the one he hoped might do him a favor, was apologetic: "Doc, we've had a run on those and our supplier hasn't been by yet."

He had ended up buying a half-pint of worms instead.

"Yep. The report was in when I stopped by my office on my way out here. Took a couple days for the Wausau boys to hear back from their firearm and toolmark examiner. But Bruce said that using a comparison microscope, the examiner was able to prove that the bullets Bruce dug out of the wood paneling on the boat as well as the two found in Bud's body during the autopsy came from the same firearm. There is no question that the rifling in the barrel, which is unique to Nancy Jarvison's .357 Smith & Wesson, matches the impressions on the bullets.

"Nancy's arrogance didn't help either," said Lew. "She never even took the trouble to wipe her prints off the gun. Hers are the only ones on it."

"So if Cynthia hadn't alerted us to that box in the linen drawer the FBI and the DEA would have assumed he was a victim of Miguel's drug cartel cronies?" asked Osborne.

"Made sense. To me, to all of us. And that conclusion made everyone's job easier so it was tempting. Of course, Nancy is convinced she'll get away with this. She's hired one of the top criminal defense attorney teams in Wisconsin."

"I suppose the real question," said Osborne looking up from his tackle box, "is can she bully a jury the way she's bullied her way through life?"

"That, dear heart, *is* the question," said Lew with a slight smile, her eyes still closed. "She's got the money to pay the lawyers. That life insurance check arrived right on schedule so she's got twenty million in the bank—or what's left after she pays off all Bud's debts."

"Yes and one other interesting note is this—remember how Cynthia thought that she may have heard fireworks that night and then she was under the impression that Nancy had called in to complain to the sheriff's department? Well, I checked yesterday and there is no record of her calling in a complaint that night. For what that's worth.

• • •

"Hey, Doc . . . do you have the cooler with sodas down there?"

The voice was Ray's, hollering down from the picnic table where he and Cody were attempting to organize Ray's fishing gear. At least Ray was trying to organize things. Cody, eyes barely visible under his "magic fish hat" was so excited that when he wasn't running in circles around Ray and the table, he was jumping up and down, elbows pumping.

"Cody . . . buddy," warned Ray, his tone gruff but friendly. "You have to settle down and help me carry these rods . . . please?"

Listening, Osborne couldn't help but think that Ray's parents, long deceased, would relish seeing their son put through the rigors he had wreaked on them. What goes around comes around.

"Yes, we have the cooler with sodas and sandwiches here on the boat," Osborne shouted back. He turned to Lew. "Can you believe that one week ago we weren't sure if that little guy would make it?"

Indeed, more information had come out in the press in recent days as there had been outbreaks of spinal meningitis on the east and west coasts with some cases resulting in loss of hearing, brain damage, and amputations. The more news Osborne saw, the more grateful he was.

"He certainly has an appetite," said Lew. "I could not believe what he ate for breakfast. Ray is an excellent cook but even so—eleven sausages, two eggs, and five pancakes! Don't let the kid fall out of the boat, Doc. He'll sink."

Twenty minutes later, as the pontoon slowed for anchoring on the edge of Ray's secret spot for big muskies, Osborne reached into his tackle box for the Styrofoam cup of worms and held it open for Cody to take one. The boy's face fell. "Baby worms, Grandpa? I thought we were going to use nightcrawlers."

"They aren't babies," said Osborne. "These are grown-up worms and they're all the bait shop had today."

"Hold on," Ray interrupted. "I've got nightcrawlers."

"You do? Where did you get 'em?" asked Osborne. "I called around to every bait shop in the county—couldn't find a single crawler."

"Ah ha," said Ray. "If you and Chief Ferris didn't retire so early . . ." His wink was so broad that Lew punched him in the shoulder. "I . . ." said Ray with a triumphant wave of his index finger "went out . . . with my flashlight . . . at midnight . . . and . . . voilà!" He reached down under the pontoon's steering wheel for a paper sack from which he pulled a large Styrofoam container. He uncapped it to expose a wriggling mass of big, fat nightcrawlers packed in dirt.

With a loud squeal, Cody bounced up and down, rocking the pontoon so severely that all three adults shouted in unison: "Settle down!" Cody giggled and did his best to sit still on one of the boat cushions.

"All right, Cody . . . watch me do this now," said Ray. "Then you can try. First, I hook the worm through the nose . . . push the barb out the bottom like this . . . and rebury the hook dead center in the nightcrawler—see? Try not to have the hook point exposed . . . when you feel a bite . . . you want to make sure you strike hard enough to move the hook into the fish's mouth."

"Let me do it," said Cody, jumping to his feet. "Please?"

"Sure, little man, your turn," said Ray, handing Cody his spinning rod with a bare hook and a sinker tied to the end of the fishing line.

After pushing back the stuffed fish hat on his head so he could see better, the little boy's face was dead serious as he knelt to work with the fishhook and the nightcrawler. When he had finished, Ray examined the result.

Cody held his breath until he heard Ray say, "Good job."

Osborne, who had been watching over his grandson's shoulder, said, "Cody, you have excellent small motor control. You work so well with your fingers—maybe you'll grow up to be a dentist."

"Oh no, Grandpa, I want to be just like Uncle Ray."

If ever a kid looked blissful as he cast his spinning rod with its big, fat nightcrawler it was Cody. He never saw the horror on his grandfather's face.